COULDA
A SECOND CHANCE FOR MR. RIGHT
BOOK ONE

PEPPER NORTH

Pepper North
With a Wink Publishing, LLC

Text copyright© 2023 Pepper North
All Rights Reserved

AUTHOR'S NOTE:

The following story is completely fictional. The characters are all over the age of 18 and as adults choose to live their lives in an age play environment.

This is a series of books that can be read in any order. You may, however, choose to read them sequentially to enjoy the characters best. Subsequent books will feature characters that appear in previous novels as well as new faces.

You can contact me on
my Pepper North Facebook pages,
at www.4peppernorth.club
eMail at 4peppernorth@gmail.com
I'm experimenting with Instagram, Twitter, and Tiktok.
Come join me everywhere!

CHAPTER 1

In the beginning

Third grade began as all years did. A class full of unique personalities and abilities burst into a cheerfully decorated room to meet their teacher and see who would be in the same class. In one particular classroom, students paused at the doorway looking for the new teacher at school. Would she be nice or strict?

Their worlds were upended when they found a quirky-looking male teacher wearing a big bow tie. Meeting them with a big smile, Mr. Chamberlain encouraged everyone to find the desk with their name on it. Clumped together in small groups, the students slowly slid into their assigned seats.

Maisie, Amber, Harper, Beau, and Colt discovered they were group five, arranged the farthest from the teacher's desk. Despite the boys giving each other cootie shots when they found out they were sitting with girls, the group bonded quickly and spent the rest of the year begging him to let them remain together. Thankfully, the phenomenal teacher responded to their good behavior and positive support for each other and hadn't separated them.

. . .

Avondale High School – Home of the Dragons
Amber

Squealing with excitement, Amber Murphy flailed her pompons as the star running back of the Dragons' football team ran out of the end zone with the football held over his head in triumph.

"You did it!" she screamed as he headed her way.

Built like a powerful machine, Colt slowed just before he reached her and wrapped one arm around Amber's waist to lift the head cheerleader into the air. Whirling in a circle, he celebrated his winning touchdown with one of his closest friends.

"We won!" he cheered, his deep voice carrying into the stands where the crowd stomped and celebrated.

"They're coming," Amber warned when she saw the entire team and coaches racing their way.

"Hold onto this for me!" he said as he set her gently on the ground before handing her the football.

Amber watched him turn to the stands and exchange an air high five with the two other members of their close-knit group. She grinned at the excitement on their faces before waving the football at the quarterback who raced forward to join the celebration. Amber knew Beau had placed that ball perfectly for Colt to snatch it from the air so skillfully.

Crap! A motion caught her eye. Seeing the cheerleading coach frantically waving her hands, Amber reached down, set the football in front of her, and grabbed her pompons as the other cheerleaders milled around, unorganized in the festivities.

"Come on, girls. Let's show them the Dragon spirit!" Amber launched into her favorite cheer and the squad followed.

Her gaze found Harper in the bleachers. Even from here, Amber could see the tears in her eyes as the curvy blonde rooted for Colt. No matter how hard Harper tried to cover her love for their friend, Amber could see right through her.

* * *

COLT

"That was a wicked run, Colt!" Maisie congratulated. "You ran like your ass was on fire."

"It had to be." Colt laughed and hugged her close for a few seconds before stepping back to look at the only people he really wanted to hang with tonight.

"I think the team wants you to come celebrate with them," Maisie pointed out as she moved away, nodding at the large gathering of athletes who chanted his name.

"I hang out with them for hours all the time. Besides, you all smell so much better," Colt said, tugging Harper to his side despite her attempts to keep her distance.

"Stay here. I want to enjoy this night with you." He looked around the small gathering on a quieter side of the bonfire, a celebration of the team's state win. "With all of you. We won't have many more of these celebrations."

"Colt, don't you want to come hang out with the Dragonettes?" Miranda inserted herself into their conversation, nodding at the dance squad she led. All the carefully made-up beauties in the elite group stared their way.

"Hi, Miranda. I'll catch up with you in art on Monday," Colt answered, nicely putting her off.

He avoided high school drama, and the cliques that spawned many of them, like the plague. Life was too short to select his friends based on their appearance, class rank, or social status. His trusted friends had bonded in third grade. It was pure coincidence that there were three girls and two boys in the group.

Now looking at the sullen face of one of the popular girls at school, Colt was glad the five of them had stuck together through thick and thin. He'd hate to rely on Miranda for support when things got tough. Colt suspected she'd bail if he got a bad haircut. He smiled at her when she didn't move away, trying to charm her into going away quietly. When she propped her hands on her hips with a huff, he knew that wouldn't happen.

"You know no one understands this group: an athlete performer, a future politician, a brainiac hick, the head cheerleader, and a fat dunce," Miranda complained spitefully when she didn't get her way.

Colt stepped in front of a bristling Amber and recoiling Harper. "Walk away, Miranda. If you were a guy, you'd be on the ground now. Since you're not, know that our casual friendship is over. I don't talk to mean girls."

"What? Fine. Just stay with your *friends*," she sneered, putting that last word in air quotes like they weren't really that as she turned and stalked away.

"What a bitch!" Amber spat and took a step to follow her.

"Whoa, Nellie." Beau hauled her back to the group with an arm around her slender waist. "She's definitely not worth our time. So, what do you think she'll do in a few months when school is out?"

"They're hiring at the Wash n Go," Harper suggested, drawing everyone's attention as she suggested Miss Popular would get a job at the rundown laundromat downtown.

"Meow!" Amber commented as her anger melted into amusement when the sweetest of their group, maybe of everyone in their class, came up with such an outlandish idea.

The sound of the group's delighted laughter rang out, drawing attention from the other students. Colt noticed several baffled expressions thrown their way. No one had ever understood how well the group fit together except Mr. Chamberlain.

"There's a reserved pool table at Murphy's for us," Amber suggested.

"Why are we hanging out here? Let's go." Colt was immediately all in. He was done hanging out with people who liked him just for scoring the winning touchdown.

When a thought flickered into life, he turned to Beau. "Think it will piss your dad off if you hang out at the bar tonight?"

"Not a chance. I rocketed that ball fifty yards before you carried it a few yards into the end zone. He'll be on the phone with every Ivy League coach everywhere, sharing footage," Beau answered with a self-deprecating laugh before hesitating. "Just don't let anyone buy us a round of beer."

"Like my dad would allow that," Amber scoffed. "Your dad's political clout, combined with the fact he'd lose his liquor license, will have him focusing a security camera on us to prove we guzzled only soft drinks all night."

"I could eat about a dozen of his giant pretzels right now," Colt confessed, rubbing his flat stomach.

"I hadn't thought of that! Training is over. Bring on the cheat meal of the century," Beau cheered. Wrapping his arms around Maisie's and Amber's waists, he steered them away from the bonfire.

"Come on, Harper. Let's go hang out with people we like," Colt suggested, pulling the curvy woman to his side.

"I'm trying to diet, Colt. Maybe it would be better if I just go home," Harper suggested.

"No way. I'll eat carrot sticks with you. Murphy's has a killer veggie tray as well." Colt cut off that suggestion and added, "You'll stay and help me celebrate, won't you?" before she could make another excuse.

"Think Rio's working tonight?" Harper asked with a meaningful look that Colt understood instantly.

"Without a doubt. We'll need to chaperone Amber. The heat building between them is scorching."

"The way she watches him," Harper commented with a knowing look. "I wonder if he'll make a move when she turns eighteen next week."

"Who knows? Maybe you'll decide to go to the movies with me next week." Colt had asked her every week since the first day of sixth grade. Harper had yet to go on a date with him.

"Alone? No way. I'd have to fend off girls wanting to feed you popcorn all night," Harper said, pantomiming one of their overly eager classmates who clustered around Colt.

"Fine. I'll just ask you out three hundred and nine more times."

"Three hundred and nine times?" she echoed.

"That's how many times I've asked you to the movies. Maybe you'll take pity on me and agree at four fifty," he joked.

"You kept track of how many times you've asked me to the movies?" Harper questioned in disbelief.

"Of course. When something is important to you, you count. Hey, wait. Why didn't I think of this?" Colt pulled out his phone and shielded the screen before typing with his thumb. Almost instantly, her phone buzzed.

Harper shot him a glance as she pulled her phone from her pocket. *Come to the movies with me.* Buzz after buzz sounded as messages bombarded her cell. Each said exactly the same thing.

"Stop!" she demanded with a laugh.

"Only one way to stop me," he warned.

"Goof. Let's go get pretzels," she suggested.

Colt squeezed her fingers and plotted how to convince Harper that they were meant to be together.

* * *

Amber

Amber climbed into the back of Beau's flashy convertible, despite Maisie's protests. "I need to think through a new cheer. I'm so tired of the old ones and basketball season is gearing up. You guys sit in the front and talk."

She watched Maisie slide into the soft leather seat and try to disappear from view. When they'd been kids, whose family made more money hadn't been important. As they'd gotten older, her sweet friend had excelled in academics, wearing the worn second- or third-hand clothing that her family could afford. It didn't make any difference to her friends, but the judgmental people in town hadn't ever let her forget just how poor her family was. Amber hadn't ever seen Maisie angry until Beau had bought her a winter coat with a month of his allowance.

"Take it back!" Maisie demanded, shoving the soft fabric jacket back at her seventh-grade friend, who waited to see her reaction to his gift.

"Don't you like the color? They had pink, too, but I thought you'd like the blue better," Beau had offered, his expression revealing his confusion.

"I don't want your charity."

"It's not charity. It's a present, Maisie. I saw it in the store and liked it. I thought you would, too," he protested. "I thought it would match your eyes."

"Stop looking at my eyes, Beau. Stop being sorry for me. I'm plenty warm," Maisie protested, visibly shivering in the cold January wind.

"Let's go inside and talk. I didn't mean to make you feel bad. I just wanted to take care of you," Beau whispered softly.

"I'm headed home. Take that back to the store. They'll give you a refund," Maisie ordered.

"I'll walk you home," Beau answered.

When they'd disappeared from Amber's view, he'd still carried the jacket, but his arm had wrapped around her waist to share his heat and block the wind. He'd walked her home every day until his father had given him a sports car for his birthday. Then Beau had driven her home despite her protests.

Amber stifled a laugh. She could still remember him driving by her side as Maisie stubbornly walked on the busy highway her brilliant friend traversed each day to get to school. She sobered, remembering Beau had shared that he'd almost gotten hit by a semi coming over a hill behind him when he'd inched forward next to Maisie. Only then had Maisie climbed into the car and allowed him to drive her the rest of the way home.

The two were perfect together. Both were brilliant. Maisie already had a full ride scholarship for an impressive university recognized by its letters alone. Beau was waiting to hear from the Ivy League schools. Watching Beau reach over the console to take Maisie's hand, Amber wondered how they'd survive without each other.

The two were so good together. Maisie's super intelligence didn't threaten Beau in the least. His thought processes could keep up with hers, at least for a while. Amber drummed her fingers on the fine leather and wondered if Beau would ever make his move to use carnal activities to distract Maisie from memorizing complex formulas. She'd intercepted Maisie's longing looks at him when Beau wasn't watching, and his aimed at Maisie. She wondered how long it would take for Maisie to admit she was interested in nonintellectual interactions.

* * *

"Sparky!" Jack Murphy called as the group walked into the packed bar. The crowd parted for the stout, affable owner as he stretched his arms wide to scoop up his daughter.

"Dad, please!" Amber protested, pushing at his chest. Everyone knew she'd given up trying to get him to stop using her childhood nickname, spawned by her fiery red hair. When he set her on her feet, she relented and kissed his cheek.

"What a run, young Colt!" Jack held out his hand to shake the athlete's hand before turning to offer it again to Beau. "I didn't miss who fired that bomb through the rushers to land as softly as a hummingbird in Colt's hands."

"Thanks, Mr. Murphy," Beau answered respectfully as he shook the older man's hand.

Amber watched her friend lean forward to hear the soft words the bar owner shared. She knew her father warned him privately about the legal letter Jack had received from Beau's congressman father, requesting that the high schooler not be allowed in the bar again. She moved closer to eavesdrop.

"It's okay. I'll deal with my father. I'm sorry he bothered you," Beau answered, with steel straightening his spine.

"He doesn't scare me much," Jack confided. "He'd lose all these votes if he closed the place down."

Beau's gaze met Amber's as her father rushed off to speak to other customers.

Sorry! she mouthed. Amber regretted not telling him of the missive delivered by courier after their last visit to the bar. Not that she thought it would surprise him or change his desire to hang out at Murphy's with the group. She was just sorry she hadn't alerted him so he wouldn't be caught off guard.

He just shrugged it off. Amber knew his father's insistence on presenting a sparkling clear profile was not something new to Beau. She suspected Beau's interaction with their diverse group had created problems for years. It made her proud of him. Beau didn't bow down to his father's demands. He loved his friends as much as they loved him.

A familiar figure approached, and she completely lost track of her thoughts. *Rio. Is there a more gorgeous man on the face of the earth?* She'd been infatuated with him since her dad had hired him—first as an honorary big brother who was always around and now as the captivating man who sent shivers down her spine.

Women flocked into the bar to flirt with the handsome bartender. Her dad said that was good for business. More women attracted more men and sold more alcohol and food.

Amber hated them all. Even now, as Rio approached, a scantily clothed woman stopped him with a hand on his bulging bicep despite the heavy tray of drinks he balanced. His response appeared cordial and charming from a distance. From the look on the woman's face as she turned around, it had also not been the one she'd wanted. Mentally, Amber thumbed her nose at her. *Better luck next time.*

Rio never took women up on their offers to date or sleep with them—or at least, Amber didn't know that he did. No ex-girlfriends showed up to cause problems. He seemed happier chatting with her at the bar during the slow times than he did talking to the glamorous women who offered him everything.

Over the years, Amber had basked in his attention. He always treated her like a favorite sibling when she visited the bar. Rio was funny and worldly. She liked his company a lot.

He'd even reserved a stool for her next to the service bar where the servers picked up their drinks. Rio would charm whoever was there to move to another seat so she could hop up and talk with him as he made drinks and prepped garnishes. He even treated her to virgin strawberry daiquiris when the bar was slow, or her version of coffee, which was laced with a ton of sugar and exactly four creams, if he was too busy to do more than pour.

The first time an image of her sitting on top of the bar wrapped in his arms had popped into her head while she was sitting there chatting with him, Amber had run away. Now, she'd dreamed it so many times, Amber could almost pretend it had happened. But, of course, it hadn't. *Yet.*

"Sodas and pretzels?" Rio asked, meeting her gaze over the crowd.

"Please! Thanks, Rio. And some veggies, too."

His smile warmed her to the core. She hadn't given up on him. Something drew her to him despite his refusal to have anything to do with her. Amber's eighteenth birthday was just around the corner. She knew he'd crumble then. Her plan hadn't jelled together yet, but Amber knew she just needed to be irresistible.

* * *

Maisie

Maisie mentally counted the change in her pocket. Whatever was on Rio's tray would have to go to another patron. She'd drink water and have just as much fun celebrating the Dragons' win with her friends.

"Root beer and goodies on Mr. Murphy for his favorite teenagers," Rio announced, stressing the beverage name distinctly and loudly for the sake of the other patrons in the bar and grill. "Go Dragons!"

"Rio, bring me water next time, okay?" Maisie whispered to the bartender. She got the distinct impression that he'd fallen on hard times during his life and would understand.

"Gotcha," the handsome bartender acknowledged with no further questions.

With that taken care of, she turned back to speak to Beau, who stayed at her side while the crowd swarmed toward Colt to congratulate him on his winning touchdown. It peeved her they didn't recognize the player who'd launched that skillful pass.

"Shouldn't they be smacking you on the butt, too?"

"I'm just part of the team. There were a lot of us on the field. Besides, hopefully, this has gotten Colt a scholarship."

Distracted by that thought, Maisie turned to look at Colt. She'd love for him to land on his feet after high school.

"Have you found a university where the professors can stimulate your brain instead of you challenging theirs?" Beau teased, drawing her attention back to him.

"I think so. They seem very cutting-edge from my interviews. I'm going to absorb all the information they can shove into my brain," she answered with a laugh.

Maisie loved her high school teachers, but she quickly exceeded their level of knowledge. Her math and science teachers had worked together to establish a link with the college they'd both attended to allow her to sit in on advanced science and applied calculus classes. She still took the same tests as others in her assigned high school classes. Maisie just didn't waste time studying things she had already mastered.

The only person she taught was Beau. His mind was so sharp. He loved science almost as much as she did, but his skills in debate and as an athlete were the talents that everyone noticed about him. She knew he would bow to his father's desire that he go to law school and then into politics. It's what his parents had groomed him to do since birth. Perhaps she could influence the future of the environment and ecology by fueling his love of science and data.

Looking at the tall teenager next to her, Maisie saw a glint of silver. She reached out to stroke the hair on his temple. "You're going gray."

"I know. It just cropped up. My dad was completely gray by age thirty. His started going silver in high school as well. He's way too happy that I'm his mini me," Beau said with a grimace.

"As if you could be anyone's mini me," Maisie protested. "You're nothing like your dad."

"I'm more similar to him than I'd like, but I do think he tries to use his political power to do the right thing. His ideas and mine differ."

"I'd say."

Changing the subject, Beau suggested, "Let's sign up Harper and Colt for karaoke."

"I know the perfect song," Maisie enthused.

Someone should be able to love the person who meant the most to them in the world. Maisie peeked up at the handsome senior next to her and tried to ignore the thought that popped into her mind.

It could never work out between an aristocratic guy from the rich side of town and a scrawny girl who has cardboard in her sneakers to make them last a few more months.

* * *

HARPER

When her name was called, Harper turned toward the door. She definitely didn't want to sing in front of this packed crowd. Colt wrapped an arm around her waist and growled into her ear.

"Come on, Angel, I can't do this without you. Help me celebrate, Harper."

"There are so many people."

"Just concentrate on me, Little girl."

Her gaze locked with his and saw the encouragement and caring in his eyes. "I hate you for making me do this," she protested.

"Come on. You'll love me when the music starts," he answered confidently.

Snorting quietly, Harper focused on the worn flooring in the bar as he coaxed her up on the small stage. Held against his powerful frame, she refused to look at the faces that stared at them. He was pure hotness and toned muscle. She knew she looked ridiculous next to him. Harper knew she outweighed him by thirty pounds, at least.

The lyrics flashed on the screen, and she forced herself to take a deep breath. His "you've got this" reassured her almost as much as the familiar music. She loved this song and hated it at the same time. Launching herself into the riveting female solo at the beginning, Harper heard the quick intake of breath from those crowded closest to her.

This was one thing she did well. Sing. She'd always loved to sing—but in the shower, in the woods, or alone with her friends at a campfire. Performing in front of other people scared her badly. Harper relied on Colt's strength as he held her steady at his side.

She relaxed a slight amount as his rich tenor voice joined hers. The crowd spontaneously clapped in appreciation. Harper glanced up at Colt and found him in the zone, making eye contact with their audience and soaking in their enjoyment. He was a complete entertainer—a combination of devastating appearance, incredible voice, charm, and the undefinable star quality. He made her tingle inside, and she'd even seen him taste the wintergreen paste back in elementary school.

That thought made her laugh inside and more of the tension ebbed from her body. Feeling it, Colt rewarded her with a squeeze of his arm as he sang just for her. Harper hadn't asked him about his plans after high school yet. She knew he wasn't ready to decide to accept an athletic scholarship at their state university. Colt seemed to wrestle with some other option he hadn't shared with her yet.

He will when he's ready.

Harper would make it through high school with the help of her friends and specially chosen classes. She toyed with taking a few business classes at the local community college next year. Her joy in life was children. Not school-age kids but little ones who smelled like baby powder, or the grass they trampled on unsteadily in the yard.

While she babysat all the neighborhood kids, Harper dreamed of opening her own childcare center—something small at first but expanding as she could. Kids were her life. She loved them whether they giggled at her lame jokes or screamed with a skinned knee. Harper knew she could make a difference for them, and she was determined to be the best second mommy to everyone she cared for.

The song ended with a reprise of her solo that had launched the song. Harper channeled all her dreams and hopes for the future into the lyrics, allowing her voice to swell into the notes. When the final sound faded out, there was absolute quiet for two seconds before thunderous applause filled the bar.

"Damn, Angel. Together, we're unbeatable." Colt's rough voice slid over her, drawing her gaze to his handsome face.

"You're the star, Colt. I just make you sound better."

Harper watched his expression harden and knew he didn't care for her words. The crowd interrupted them with demands for an encore and she quickly keyed in a tune that required two male voices. Waving Beau up to take her place, she fled from the stage to rejoin Maisie and Amber. Ignoring the feel of Colt's gaze on her, she chatted with her friends as the masculine tones blended together. Beau's voice was good. Colt's voice was incomparable.

* * *

Rio

Rio wiped the sticky countertop and avoided the feminine hands that reached out to touch him. He knew women found him attractive, but he wanted something special from a relationship. Catching Amber's knowing look, he shook his head at her. She'd amused him as a perky kid when he'd started at the bar in his late teens. As Amber had grown up, that enjoyment of interacting with a fun-loving kid had morphed into watching her become an amazing adult.

Now at thirty-one, he kept his distance from her. Because he'd been in her life so long, she naturally flirted with him as she tried out her feminine wiles. Maintaining their buddy relationship, Rio hadn't had trouble remembering that she was a kid. *Until recently.*

As her eighteenth birthday approached, Rio wanted her to enjoy her final high school year as he never could—to be a kid for as long as possible. Leaning on the bar, Rio relaxed his guard and allowed himself to watch the pleasure on Amber's face as she listened to Colt and Harper's incredible duet.

"She's off limits, Rio," Jack Murphy growled in his ear before continuing, "Don't touch Sparky. She's going to college to become a nurse and live an incredible life out there." His boss nodded at the front door. "I don't care if she is eighteen next month. Stay away from her or you'll be out on your ear."

"Got it, boss. Amber and I are buddies. Nothing more," Rio assured him with an easy smile he'd practiced for years.

"You're smart for a guy who walked in here with the ink still wet on his bartending license. I wrestled with hiring an eighteen-year-old, but the ladies love you. I still don't see how you can pinpoint accounting issues by simply glancing at invoices. You're a boon to Murphy's, but..."

"I won't forget—Amber's off limits," Rio finished the statement for him.

"That table over there needs another pitcher of margaritas," Jack said, patting him on the back.

"On it, boss."

He allowed himself to watch Amber congratulate her friends as they stepped off the stage. Rio knew Amber had something planned for her eighteenth birthday. He better figure out some way to disrupt her plans. If not, she'd never understand.

CHAPTER 2

Amber bounced through the kitchen door with a smile plastered on her face. She'd had a great birthday at school, celebrating with her friends. Harper had even brought Amber's favorite molten chocolate cupcakes to school for lunch.

"Hi, baby! You look happy!" Amber's mom, Gretchen, greeted her as she swapped out laundry.

"I am. Only one more thing could make my day even better."

"Your dad isn't going to buy you that red, hopped-up sports car," Gretchen warned.

"I know. Besides, I'd want a purple one. That would be much prettier."

"Not that one, either," Gretchen told her with a waggle of her index finger. "But there might be a letter on the island for you."

"No way!" Amber raced to pluck the official-looking letter from the granite countertop. She grabbed the letter opener from the drawer and carefully sliced open the top.

Extracting the letter inside, Amber silently read the embossed letters at the top. This had been her reach school. The one she'd been sure she would never be chosen to attend. Quickly, she read the missive aloud for her mother, who now stood next to her with an arm wrapped around Amber's waist.

"You made it in! Congratulations. Your father is going to be so proud. You should drive to the bar and show him," Gretchen suggested.

"On my way!"

Amber grabbed her keys from the hook by the door and drove her sensible compact to Murphy's. This was a slow time in the afternoon. The lunch crowd would have cleared out except for a few diehards and the happy hour celebrants would still be at work.

Walking in the front door, Amber spotted Rio slicing lemons and limes into wedges for the bar. She stopped in her tracks. The university nursing program was in Durham, North Carolina. She'd be states away from Rio.

His head lifted and she darted out of view before he could see her. Suddenly, the dream nursing school seemed like an impediment rather than something to be excited about. Her heart pounded inside her chest. How would she choose? The university or Rio?

"Sparky!" Amber's father's gravelly voice made her jump. "I wondered where you were. Your mom just texted to see if you'd told me. She sounded excited. What's up?"

"Dad!"

"What's that?" he asked, pointing at the letter in her hand. "Does that say what I think it does?"

Torn by her desires, Amber could only nod.

"May the saints be praised!" Murphy rushed forward to wrap his arms around her waist and whirl the two of them in a tight circle, just as he'd done with her when she was two. "You did it, Sparky. All the time you studied after games, all those sessions where your mom quizzed you over biology, and signing up for every challenging class you could take—it all added up to setting yourself up for the best future ever."

Unable to prevent herself, Amber looked over his shoulder at Rio, who now leaned against the door frame. Their gazes meshed, and he said softly, "Happy birthday, Little girl."

He'd never called her that before. Amber had gotten used to Brat, Amberella, Ella, and of course, her name, coming from his lips over the years. She'd never heard him call her that before. *Little girl.* Unable to look away from his knowing eyes, Amber felt those words resonate inside her. She felt something click into place.

"Back to work, Rio. Just a private celebration here. Amber just got accepted into the best damn nursing program available. She'll go to North Carolina in a few months," Murphy interrupted gruffly.

Amber had never heard her father speak to the long-time bartender like that. Rio had been around long enough to be considered family. She pushed away from her father, embarrassed by his tone.

"Thank you, Rio," she answered, attempting to send him an apology with her gaze.

"You're welcome, Amber. And congratulations on the news."

Without another word, Rio turned and walked toward the bar. Instantly, several customers called his name and lifted their glasses. Jumping over the bar in his traditional athletic practice, the handsome bartender drew applause from the women who clustered in front of him. Amber grimaced to see a couple adjust the neckline of their plunging T-shirts lower to attract his attention.

"You're not to associate with Rio, Amber. He's a handsome guy, but you're meant for better things. Stay away from him." Murphy spoke harshly.

"Dad! What are you talking about? Rio's worked for us forever."

"Exactly. He's an employee. That's all."

Amber shook her head and looked down at the letter in her hand. Only a small zing of excitement zipped through her now at the triumph of landing the exclusive spot in the challenging nursing program. She still wanted to go, but now she was torn.

"I know, Sparky. It's tough growing up and making the right choices. Going to North Carolina will be exciting and scary at the same time. I have a feeling you'll find a new posse of friends and maybe even someone special there," her father suggested, as if he'd read her mind.

"I like my friends here," she argued.

"They'll still be your friends. The only person who I haven't heard is going somewhere after graduation is Harper," he reminded her.

When Amber nodded, he added, "Don't you want to share your news with them?"

"I guess. Dad, I don't understand. You told me to stay away from Rio when I was younger. I get that. I didn't want to cause problems for him. But I'm eighteen now…"

"And you're still too young. Don't cost the man his job, Sparky. You'll lose interest too quickly, anyway. What's the longest you've ever dated anyone? Four weeks? Is that worth his livelihood?" her father interrupted to point out.

"Dad!"

"Go tell your friends and think about what I've said. I think you'll decide this old man may be right."

* * *

"WHAT'S WRONG?" Harper asked later that evening as the group minus Colt gathered in her basement. He had run home to shower before coming over. Thank goodness.

Maisie and Beau huddled together, studying for an advanced lit test they had tomorrow. From the number of books scattered around them that they frantically thumbed through, it would be a hairy exam.

"Dad warned me off Rio. I've never heard him talk like that."

"And you couldn't charm him out of being suspicious? You usually have men eating out of your hand," Harper said with a meaningful look.

"I do not."

"Girl…"

"Okay, I get my share of attention, but Rio's always been Rio. Like he's a part of the family. Besides, he's got a thousand women lined up at the bar ready to hook up. I can't compete with that," Amber pointed out.

"Of course you can."

"Can I tell you something to keep between you and me?" Amber watched Harper nod before continuing, "He called me something today. I hadn't ever heard it except in that book."

"Really? What was it?"

"Little girl."

Amber could see from the expression that flashed over Harper's face that her friend instantly remembered the book they'd shared back and forth until it was literally falling apart. It had disappeared from Amber's pile of books one evening at the bar.

"Like *the* book?" Harper whispered.

Immediately, Beau's chin lifted, and he tuned into their conversation. "The book?" he echoed. "The one I found in the parking lot on my way into school?"

"Yes," Amber admitted, feeling her face heat a bit.

"I thought we decided to not talk about that book aloud ever again. We just write our notes in the margins," Maisie pointed out, drumming her fingers on the literature they were neglecting.

"Rio called Amber 'Little girl' today," Harper shared.

"You were supposed to keep that between you and me," Amber hissed, throwing her hands up in the air dramatically.

"Come on! Harper can't keep a secret. You wanted us to know," Beau pointed out.

"Hey!" Harper protested Beau's assessment before slumping in her chair. "You're right. I can't keep a secret from any of you."

"Should we wait until Colt is here?" Beau asked.

"I'm here. What are we waiting for?" Colt appeared at the bottom of the stairs with a supersized pizza.

"That's it! Time for a break," Maisie declared, carefully moving the textbooks away to protect them.

A few minutes later, the pizza box lay open on the coffee table between them, and everyone munched a slice of pepperoni heaven. Amber hoped that her friends had forgotten what they'd discussed when Colt arrived, but she should have known better.

"So…catch me up," Colt demanded.

"Rio called Amber *Little girl*," Harper provided as she nibbled on the crust of the smallest piece of pizza.

"Harper!" Amber protested again.

"What? Everyone else knew," Harper defended herself.

"He did?" Colt's attention switched from the slice in his hand to Amber. "What did he say exactly?"

"Happy birthday, Little girl," Amber admitted.

"We knew others had to exist—Daddies and Little girls! Do you think Rio is a Daddy?" Beau asked.

"Definitely," Maisie answered. "I've known that for a while."

"What?" Amber screeched and then lowered her voice as she heard Harper's dad stomp three times on the floor above them. That signal meant quiet. When he flipped the lights three times on the stairs, it was time for everyone to go home. They all paid attention to her friend's dad. He was a massive man who worked for the state highway department driving an excavator.

"Sorry!" she whispered. "You can't just say that and not explain. What are you talking about, Maisie?"

"I've suspected Rio was a Daddy for a while. I finally just asked him," Maisie explained.

"What? You just asked him? Like… Hey, Rio. Are you a Daddy?" Amber mocked, unbelieving.

"It was more like… Rio, I think you're a Daddy dom. Am I wrong?" Maisie said bluntly.

Beau covered his mouth and Amber knew he was trying not to laugh. Maisie sometimes didn't have a polite filter. Blurting out random bits of information or questions was part of her charm. It was as if she was too busy solving the complex problems in her mind to worry about social acceptability.

Colt raised an eyebrow and nodded. "That would be the most direct way to find out. What did he say?"

"Yes." Maisie took another bite of pizza and chewed as she looked around at everyone leaning forward eagerly.

"That's all? He just said yes, and you didn't ask him any other follow-up questions?" Amber asked, trying to keep her volume down so they didn't get another quieting stomp from Harper's dad.

"That was the only thing I wanted to know." When Amber tumbled dramatically to the floor, Maisie asked, "What? I didn't have like prewritten questions. I was sitting at the bar waiting while you were in the bathroom and the question popped into my mind."

"When was this?" Amber asked as she dragged herself up to sit against the side of the couch.

"I think it was before that big football game against the Chargers last year," Maisie said after thinking about it for a while.

"Like a year ago?" Harper asked.

"Probably?"

"I'm implementing a new rule now. Anyone talks to Rio about being a Daddy, I want to know," Amber stated.

"For how long?" Colt asked.

"Forever. The new rule is if you talk to Rio about being a Daddy anytime from now until we all are fifty or dead, you have to tell me." Amber looked around the circle of friends and waited for each one to nod.

CHAPTER 3

Rio knelt on the hardwood floor in his one-room apartment. Opening the battered wooden lid of his footlocker, he unpacked a few treasured mementos. At the very bottom sat a tattered volume wrapped in brown shipping paper. Carefully, he lifted the packet and removed the protective covering.

Amber always sat her books on the corner of the bar when she came in after school to talk to her dad or beg a ride to an event. He'd moved them once when a tipsy patron had almost coated her algebra book in bourbon. Over the years, it had become a habit. He liked taking care of her.

When he'd found her books on a table in the corner one evening as he was cleaning up, Rio had picked up the stack and noticed one wasn't a textbook. Carrying them to the shelf he'd established for her books, he read the spine. It said simply, *Daddy*.

Jolting to a stop, he'd looked around before setting down the pile to extricate the tattered one. After one look at the cover and scanning the blurb, Rio confirmed what he'd always suspected but tried to ignore. If reading this book was a good indication, Amber was a Little girl.

A hint of blue on one page made him turn to that location. In the margin, she'd written,

Daddies make their Littles feel safe and secure. What an amazing thing to experience! I want this. Amber

There were notes from Harper and Maisie as well as Beau and Colt. Rio knew that the book disappearing with their thoughts and names pinpointed on the pages would panic the tightly bonded group, but he needed time to read her comments. Without allowing himself to second-guess his decision, Rio left the other books where he'd found them and tucked the 'Daddy' book in a mound of boxes to take out to the dumpster. Carrying it outside, he placed it in the saddlebag of his battered motorcycle to read later.

"Rio, did you move my books? Or one of them?" Amber asked the next day after school when she rushed in with her friends. He could tell she was nervous from the way she couldn't meet his gaze.

"No. If you leave them on the bar, I tuck them underneath. Did you check there?" he asked, watching her reaction.

"I did. I left them in a different spot last night. Everything is there except for one book I need. Do you think someone else would have moved it?" she suggested.

"I doubt it. It's been pretty dead in here all day. Maybe you left that one in your locker by mistake."

"Maybe?" she answered with a skeptical expression. Amber looked over her shoulder at the group scattered behind her.

Rio found the entire group's reaction to his words telling. This meant a lot to them. Their bond had astounded him. Rio had gotten to know all of them as they'd trailed Amber into the bar. Now the mystery of how they all fit together so perfectly clicked into place like the pieces of a puzzle—something more dynamic than simple school friendships drew them together.

Rio had debated returning the book to Amber. He'd made his first slip when he'd called her Little girl. The shocked look in her eyes had made him want to hug her close and reassure Amber that everything was going to be alright—even better than alright—but he didn't have that luxury.

Allowing himself time to enjoy the sweet notes that she'd jotted in the book, Rio dreamed of a life where he could claim her as his. If only he wasn't so much older. Thirteen years' difference wouldn't be earth-shattering if he were fifty and Amber thirty-seven. Shaking his head, Rio carefully rewrapped the book and grabbed the cardboard box he'd brought it home in. Adding a gift he'd already bought her for graduation and a letter that took time to craft, Rio sealed it securely and wrote her name on the front.

She would be better off at her fancy school getting the nursing degree she'd already decided on when he'd first met her. Unlike other teenagers, Amber's goals had never wavered. Rio was proud of her.

*　*　*

"Hey, Dad. Why are you behind the bar?" Amber questioned, spotting him hard at work.

"Rio took off. An emergency of some kind," Jack answered as he filled orders.

"Oh, no! He'll be back tomorrow?"

"No. He's left town for a while. I've told him I'd welcome him back at any time."

"Left town?" Amber echoed as she climbed weakly onto a stool.

"Yes. Like I said he had some kind of emergency out of town. He left you a graduation present in that cubby where he always stashed your books," her father said, waving his hand under the bar.

Sliding behind the bar, Amber stayed out of his way as she retrieved the package and hugged it to her chest. "This was nice of him," she said when her dad looked at her expectantly.

"Aren't you going to open it?"

Scrambling for an excuse to unwrap it in private, Amber answered, "I haven't graduated yet."

"I don't think he'll know."

"I will. I'll take it home. It will inspire me to pass this calculus test tomorrow." She purposefully distracted her father as he loaded the server's tray.

"What are you doing here? Go study!" Jack ordered his daughter.

"On my way!"

Escaping to her car, Amber ripped the package open and found three items inside. Opening the sealed envelope carefully, she read Rio's precise block letters:

Little girl,

The worst thing a Daddy can do is stand in the way of someone's potential. You have so many gifts to share with the world that I'm confident you are going to be an amazing nurse. Know that wherever we are in the world, I'm sending you support and encouragement. Rock your life, Amber.

Rio

Amber read that message three times, trying to understand that he was gone. Did he leave because of some altruistic desire to help her? *How screwed up is that!*

Her eyes lingered on the words Little girl and Daddy. There was no mistaking his meaning. Amber shook her head in disbelief. She'd planned to talk to him after she graduated. There were just a few more weeks.

Numb, she folded the letter and tucked it back into the envelope. Picking up the heavy, paper-wrapped bundle, Amber unfolded it and swallowed hard. He had found it. The book Beau had found that they'd all pored over. Rio knew all her deepest thoughts.

A dreadful thought crossed her mind. Had he left because she'd disgusted him? She tore the letter back out from the envelope to reread it. As much as she tried to sense something negative from his words, Amber knew Rio hadn't judged her harshly.

She smoothed the wrinkles from the note and returned it once again to the envelope. That discussion with Maisie and her friends about Rio being a Daddy reverberated in her memories. He didn't say it, but Amber suspected he'd left because he was too old for her. That must mean he had feelings for her, right?

The final item was light and squishy to the touch. Amber tried to open it without tearing the paper. When green plush poked through the paper, she abandoned her attempt to be careful and ripped the remaining paper open. Discovering a stuffie shaped like all the lime wedges she'd watched Rio slice throughout the years, Amber squeezed it to her heart and allowed the tears welling in her eyes to tumble down her cheeks.

"Damn you, Rio. You didn't have to leave," she stormed aloud into the car. But inside, she knew dividing her attention between her studies and a long-distance relationship would have been super challenging.

Shaking away those thoughts, she texted Harper.

He's gone.

Who?

Rio. He left the book and a note.

He'll be back?

I don't think so.

Can you drive here? I need to hug you.

On my way. Can you text everyone?

I've got you.

Tucking the stuffie in her large backpack, Amber turned on the car and forced herself to focus on navigating to her friend's house.

CHAPTER 4

Prior to the fifth reunion

"I can't believe none of us can make it to the five-year reunion," Amber bemoaned on the video call with the four people she missed every day. There was one more, but he'd disappeared without leaving a trace.

"It's a long way from your latest hospital job," Beau observed. "How did you end up working in Alaska?"

"When they told me there are more men than women here, I jumped at a chance to work here," Amber joked. "They just didn't tell me a bunch of those guys live out in the bush. It's beautiful here. I just have two months more of my contract."

"I didn't like those people in high school. I can't figure out why I'd want to leave an exciting experiment to go see who married who," Maisie commented.

"They weren't all bad. Harper's still there," Beau pointed out.

"She's a glutton for punishment," Maisie replied before addressing their famous friend. "Colt? Are you on tour?"

"Sorry for the background noise. I tried to find a quiet spot," Colt apologized, taking off his cowboy hat to fan himself.

"Alabama in July isn't where I'd choose to play an outdoor venue," Beau put in.

"I'm getting used to the amount of water I need to drink to stay hydrated. It's crazy. Who knows where this rollercoaster is going to end? I'm riding the wave of popularity from my last release as long as possible," Colt answered. "In this business, it's easy for people to forget your name, even with a few hit songs."

"I saw you on the news," Harper shared. "You and Beau are the hometown heroes. Everyone is so proud of you. If they had any idea what Maisie was doing, they'd name the new library after her. I suggested it but…"

"No one is going to name a library after me unless I win a Nobel Peace Prize or something," Maisie scoffed before asking, "How are your plans to run your own daycare?"

"It's hard. I'm working and learning at the biggest one in town now. It's too industrial for what I want to do but the owner is teaching me how to keep the books and make a profit. She knows I won't compete with her whenever I have enough to open my own place," Harper confided.

"Are you taking time to sing at Murphy's?" Colt asked.

"Oh, no. My singing days are pretty well over. I just entertain toddlers nowadays," Harper said, smiling at Colt.

"That invitation is still open for you to come join me whenever you want—even for a day or two. I can send you plane tickets," he urged.

"You're too nice. You have professional backup singers now, Colt," Harper reminded him.

She quickly changed the conversation to ask Beau, "When's your next debate? The news of you running for office is buzzing around town."

"I bet. It surprised me too. Things moved quickly when the current representative decided to retire," he replied.

"Are you going to the reunion, Harper, since you're in town?" Beau asked.

"Oh, no. I'm avoiding Miranda like the plague," Harper confessed.

"Don't let her keep you from going," Amber urged.

"I won't. It's just not important without you guys there. Everyone else I see at the grocery store or church," Harper explained.

"Next time, Harper. We'll all make plans to be there for the tenth," Colt assured her.

Prior to the *tenth reunion*

"They sweet-talked me into extending my contract here in Florida for six more months. They're understaffed and I always like money. What's everyone else's excuse for not going?" Amber joked.

"I had every intention of getting there. Unfortunately, the bill I'm sponsoring is floundering and the only chance of getting it passed is by meeting with those in opposition one by one," Beau shared.

"Are you talking about the one for funding for free mammograms for those under a certain income level?" Maisie asked.

No one commented on the tears shining unshed in her eyes. Maisie's mother passed away about a year ago. She'd ignored the lump in her breast and without health insurance, she knew the test would be more expensive than she'd considered it beneficial to get. By the time she collapsed, the prognosis had been dire. Maisie hadn't been able to talk her into trying to fight. Her mom hadn't had the strength or the willingness to leave her family with a burden of debt.

"Yes. That's the one."

"I should have left the think tank and gone to work in the private sector," Maisie whispered, shaking her head.

"Stop that. Maybe that would have been an option if they'd caught it early. Your mom didn't want anyone to know. By the time you found out, it was too late. You need to stop beating yourself up," Harper chided her.

"That's easy for you to say," Maisie muttered.

"Just imagine if it was my mom or Amber's. They might have had all the testing and still decided that it was too much to undergo surgery, chemo, and radiation," Harper reminded her. "No one gets to make that decision except for the person affected by the disease."

"I know. She probably wouldn't have chosen to have anything done, regardless. Mom hated doctors' offices and being poked and prodded. It would have been her worst nightmare to go through those treatments," Maisie admitted, dashing away the tears.

"I do appreciate you helping others in her position, Beau. Maybe having you in politics isn't a waste of your intelligence after all," she teased.

"He's not just going to try. I bet you next month we all have champagne to toast his win," Amber predicted.

"Like I can afford that on my stipend," Maisie laughed.

"I'll make sure everyone has champagne if I pull this off. I'll be glad to celebrate," Beau assured her.

"That will be one thing I'll let you do for me," Maisie said to him, looking fierce. "Thank you, Beau. Regardless of how it turns out, I appreciate you trying."

"Of course. I'm counting on all of you to keep me focused on what's important," he told them.

"Where are you, Colt?" Amber asked.

"Currently, I'm in Nashville. We're fighting with the last couple of songs on this album. The record label has a different view of where it needs to go than I do," Colt reported.

"Who's going to win?" Harper asked quietly.

"Me, of course. I'd be glad to have reinforcements if you want to come yell at them for me, Harper." They all laughed. Colt always had a way of asking her to come see him.

"I don't want to duke it out with that hard-looking brunette I saw you with on the award show," Harper said with an audibly forced laugh.

"She's in a duet with me. Mirabelle is married with three kids and a bunch of baby goats. You're safe," he reported with a reproving look.

Amber could feel the tension buzzing between them, even through the video connection. "Okay, so we'll all be at fifteen now?"

"Definitely," Colt insisted.

"On my schedule," Beau added.

"I'll try my best," Maisie said and added, "I should be in a different place in five years."

"I'll be here," Harper pointed out.

"Me, too," Amber assured everyone.

Prior to the fifteenth reunion

"This is getting ridiculous," Amber said, throwing up her arms as they all looked sheepishly at each other. "That's it. We're all going to be at the twentieth. Pinky swear with me that none of us will have excuses." She held her bent little finger up to the screen and peeked around her hand to make sure everyone followed suit.

"Okay, that's a rock-solid promise no one can break," she said, reminding them all of Mr. Chamberlain's lesson in the third grade about the different types of promises and which ones to never break.

"I saw Mr. Chamberlain last week at guest story time at daycare. He wanted to know how everyone was," Harper reported.

"He wrote me an email when they published my study on bioidentical organ replacements," Maisie shared. "Do you get to see him often?"

"He comes whenever I call to fill in for a parent who cancels at the last minute," Harper answered.

"We were lucky to be in his class. He's retired now?" Beau asked.

"Yes. He retired last year. He misses the kids. You can see that," Harper informed him.

"The best teacher ever," Maisie added.

"Of all the brilliant minds you've studied with?" Colt asked in disbelief.

"In his own way, yes. He helped me survive the tough years after elementary school by equipping me with the best friends ever," she explained.

"I'll echo that. The music world is crazy. Knowing we still talk once a month keeps me sane," Colt agreed.

"Should we stop talking to each other for six months before the reunion next time, just so we have to get there?" Amber suggested.

"No's echoed from everyone.

"Then we all make the commitment that we're going to be there now," Amber stressed.

"I'll be there," Beau answered.

"I'll be there," Maisie promised.

"I'll be here," Harper tweaked the phrase, making them laugh.

"I'll be there," Colt promised. "I miss home more as time goes on."

"I'll be there, too. I'm not breaking a pinky promise. That has to be years of bad luck," Amber reminded them as she made herself a note. She'd block out six months before the reunion to make sure she was in town. She was tiring of always being on the move. Maybe it was time for her to move back to the only real home she'd ever had. Too bad her friends couldn't be there, too. Or even…

"Ever hear from Rio?" Harper asked, reading her mind.

"Not a word. You'd think I'd stop missing him," Amber lamented.

"We were all sure we'd find our Little girls and Daddies. Maybe they don't exist," Maisie suggested.

"They exist. Some of us just refuse to admit it," Beau said pointedly.

"Like you could be a Daddy with your position," she answered. "You'll probably be the president by the next reunion."

"I have always been a Daddy. I've just not had a Little girl," Beau said softly with steel in his words.

"Ditto," Colt echoed.

"Enough seriousness, guys. Everyone tell us something funny that happened to you this week. Harper, you start, and no strange objects shoved up a toddler's nose," Amber warned as Harper opened her mouth.

"Crap. You go first, Colt. Amber just vetoed my story," Harper complained with a laugh.

"So, I'm on the tour bus and I look out to see, *Hi, Colt!* written in strange letters formed by something on the ground. I'd just figured out it was material when I saw the three naked fans."

"Good-looking girls?" Harper said sharply.

"Two men and a potbellied pig," Colt answered.

"What was the pig wearing?" Maisie asked.

"Nothing but a smile," Colt reported, making them all dissolve into delighted laughter.

I miss them all so much.

CHAPTER 5

The twentieth reunion

AMBER PULLED into the parking lot of Murphy's. Crossing her fingers, she hoped everyone would be able to make it this year. They'd said they would be there but until she saw them, Amber wouldn't believe it even with the pinky swears that served as a solid contract.

Their twentieth high school reunion was a big deal. It seemed so long ago that she'd dragged herself through those last weeks of classes and thrown herself into preparations for college.

After graduation, everyone had scattered in different directions except for Harper; it had been difficult to stay in touch, but they'd all made the commitment to talk once a month. They were in such different places in their lives but, remarkably, were still the same people she'd trusted more than anyone else since third grade. She'd never seen them like others did—the politician, the brilliant biomedical engineer, the daycare worker, the country superstar.

She crossed her fingers, hoping everyone wouldn't be too star-struck for Colt to relax and enjoy some time off or eager to debate politics with Beau.

A knock on her window made her jump. Throwing her door open, Amber jumped out of the car to hug the sweet woman standing next to her. "Harper! I've missed you so much."

"Silly! We've had video chats practically every week," Harper reminded her, and squeezed her friend a bit tighter before stepping back.

"That's not the same. Where's everyone?" she asked.

"They'll be here soon. Have you been home to talk to your parents?" Harper asked with a strange sideways glance that put Amber on alert.

"I was running late. Dad's here, right? I want to ask him for a strawberry daiquiri. It still kills him to serve me alcohol. Somehow, they've missed me turning thirty-eight."

"I know. My folks still think I'm twelve," Harper shared.

Amber looked over Harper's appearance, noting her cute sundress, sandals, makeup. "Do you think I look okay? I figured rumpled jeans are a fashion statement, but you look amazing. Did I miss dress-up requirements in the schedule of events? I know, I'll put on my vamp shoes. They're in the back."

"You look gorgeous in everything," Harper assured her as Amber rustled through the trunk.

Silence stretched between them as Amber spiffed up her outfit with the killer stilettos until Harper blurted, "There's something you should know before you go inside. Want to call your folks and tell them you're here?"

"You tell me," Amber ordered in her stern—don't mess with me—nurse voice.

"Well… Let's go inside and get that daiquiri first."

"What in the world's going on? Are you okay?" When Harper nodded her head, Amber checked, "Is everyone else okay?"

"Everyone is great. In fine form," Harper rushed to assure her as she guided Amber into the bar.

"Wow! I hope everyone has a nametag. I don't recognize anyone. They all got old," Amber whispered to Harper as she looked around.

Checking for her dad at the crowded bar, Amber froze and clenched Harper's fingers as her eyes locked on a handsome figure behind the bar.

"I think I'm hallucinating."

As Harper leaned in to whisper something in her ear, the bartender looked up. Rio. It was him. His hair was silvery black under the bar lighting.

"Rio?" she whispered to no one in particular.

She recognized her name on his lips in response as he spotted her. In a familiar surge of muscles and pure masculine power, Rio braced his hands on top of the bar and vaulted over it in a display of strength and grace that drew everyone's attention. As he stalked forward, their gazes locked together.

"Amber," Rio exclaimed, running his hands down her arms as if he needed to touch her to reassure himself she was real.

He studied her face before glancing at her bare left hand. "I am so glad to see you."

"What are you doing here, Rio? Are you back working behind the bar?" she questioned.

Rio laughed and nodded ruefully. "I enjoy working behind that bar. It feels good—familiar. And you're here."

"I just accepted a job at the hospital," Amber blurted, then looked around for Harper. She hadn't told anyone yet. Amber had saved the news for a surprise.

"Congratulations." He studied her face before adding, "Your folks didn't tell you, did they?"

"What? Are they okay? Is that why you're here?"

"I think they're probably better than we are. Your dad told me they were going on a ten-day cruise through the Mediterranean Sea."

"They never leave the bar for the weekend," Amber said in shock.

"Now they can. Go talk to your friends. Then, come see me," Rio directed with a steely tone in his voice.

"You won't disappear?" she challenged.

"I won't."

Amber paused to watch him walk away. Could he have gotten hotter? When her friend cleared her throat, Amber shook off the fog surrounding her.

"What is going on?" Amber asked Harper.

"You've missed a few things. Come on. You can protect me as we pick up our nametags from Miranda. She can't resist pointing out how wonderful her life is compared to mine," Harper sighed as she guided Amber forward to the woman behind the desk, who watched them closely.

"Hi, Miranda. I hope Cinderella is feeling better," Harper commented.

"She gets so many germs at daycare. Can't you clean more to kill all the stuff the kids pass around?" Miranda complained.

"There are not enough disinfectant wipes in the world to combat the number of germs one toddler can discover," Harper joked.

"You really should take this more seriously. The city could send in inspectors," Miranda said with one arched eyebrow.

"They visit regularly. Perhaps you would prefer another daycare option. I'll miss Cinderella but completely understand." Harper stood her ground.

"If you weren't the cheapest place in town, I'd move her," Miranda snapped.

"Wow," Amber interjected, staring the unpleasant woman down. She didn't want to make a scene, but she wouldn't allow Miranda to treat Harper like this.

"It's okay, Amber. Let's just get our nametags," Harper urged, and ran a finger over the display to find hers.

Amber leaned forward to pick hers and whispered to Miranda as she pointed to two places on her hairline, "Your facelift tape is coming undone here and here."

"Well, I never," Miranda sputtered as she raised her hands to run her fingers over the spots Amber had indicated.

Amber just smiled and pulled the back off her sticker. "Just trying to help," she told the unpleasant woman as she walked away without looking back.

Instantly, the cheerleaders swarmed Amber to give her hugs and get caught up. Amber was pleased to see them include Harper in their conversation. *Thank goodness some people grow up!*

"We love the changes Rio has made to the bar. He's keeping the traditional feel but updating it," Suzanne commented.

"It is lovely," Amber started before processing Suzanne's words. Was he the new manager?

"Someone asked him at the bar if he'd change the name now that your parents retired and sold the business," another classmate shared.

"And what did he say?" Amber asked, turning around to search for Rio behind the bar. He'd deliberately let her think he was just working behind the bar.

Rio's gaze met hers. The sternness in his demeanor made her stand taller. Slowly, he shook his head. Amber returned his warning with a small, dismissive gesture. He wasn't in charge of her. Instantly, she knew that had been the wrong thing to do.

"Your strawberry daiquiri," a waitress at her elbow commented.

Amber broke her connected gaze with Rio to look at the frosty glass and then back at the young, smiling woman. "Thank you," she answered on autopilot.

"Harper, Rio sent you your favorite—a vanilla rum and diet Coke," she announced, handing over the other glass.

"Thank him for me, Monica," Harper said sweetly.

"That daiquiri looks so good. I'm off to sweet talk Rio into making one for me," one of her cheer squad members said as she walked away. The others streamed after her.

After taking a sip of her strawberry concoction, Amber slapped her hand over her mouth as laughter burst from her lips. He'd sent her a drink with no alcohol, just as he'd always done when she was a kid. Merriment glittered in her eyes as she met Rio's glance once again.

"Look, there's Maisie and Beau. He picked her up at the airport," Harper said as she pointed toward the door. A second later, she was on the move, followed closely by Amber.

"Maisie! Beau! You both look so good. Love the silver fox look, Beau. And Maisie, you could have stepped right off the cover of *Vogue*," Amber shared before pulling the slight figure in for a hug.

"Thank goodness I have a wardrobe person who picks out clothes for me. Otherwise, I'd wear a lab coat with jeans," Maisie said with a laugh.

"Now you, Harper, look like a million bucks. How can you have kids drooling over you all day long and still have that sweet look on your face?" Maisie wondered as she embraced Harper.

"Oh, you're just being nice. I'm so glad to see you both," Harper cheered, and gave Beau a bear hug before pulling back awkwardly. "Sorry. Is it bad to touch you?"

"Touch me?" Beau echoed, looking confused.

"She's worried about the media that buzzes you like a hornet's nest," Maisie guessed tartly.

"You can hug me anytime, Harper. Come here, you," Beau said to Amber and pulled her close.

"Well, well, well. The gang's all here. Except for the famous country star. He's too busy to come, I guess. Like Harper's imaginary boyfriend," Miranda's acerbic voice observed from behind them.

"Good grief, are you still so constipated that you treat people like shit?" Maisie's voice carried over the crowd.

"It's okay, Maisie. I don't know why Miranda is so worried about *my* love life." Harper didn't say anymore, but from the steam rising from Miranda's carefully stretched face, she'd struck a nerve.

A flurry of motion at the door signaled the arrival of someone who everyone remembered. Colt paused just inside the doors to search for someone. Spotting Harper, he made a beeline to her side.

"Hi, Angel." Colt wrapped his arms around Harper without looking at anyone else, pulled her into his arms, and pressed his lips to hers. "I'm sorry I am late."

Amber's eyelashes almost sizzled away from the heat of that kiss he apologized to Harper with. *What is going on?*

She looked at Maisie and Beau to judge their reaction and would have loved a picture of Maisie's gaping mouth and Beau's complete lack of reaction. *He really has this politician thing down.*

When he lifted his head, Colt shared, "The tour bus driver got slowed down by the traffic on the highway. I was about ready to jump out and run when it finally cleared."

"Colt Ziegler is your imaginary boyfriend?" Miranda gasped in shock before shaking her head. "I don't buy that!"

"Sorry?" Colt looked at her with confusion written on his face. "Are you one of our class?" He even scanned her nametag and no recognition showed on his face.

"Colt! I'm Miranda Teasdale. I led the Dragonettes."

"I thought Amber was the head cheerleader," Colt answered with a shake of his head.

"The Dragonettes. I led the dance team," Miranda retorted.

"Oh. That makes sense. I was always in the locker room when you all did your thing," Colt said dismissively before turning to shake Beau's hand. His broad shoulders blocked Miranda from the group.

"I've been watching the polls. It looks like you are a shoo-in for the Senate," Colt congratulated him, ignoring the woman behind him.

"Keep your fingers crossed for me, Colt. It's good to see you in person rather than on TV," Beau answered with a smile.

"And you two! Are you finally moving home?" Colt asked, stepping forward to hug Maisie and Amber before returning to Harper and pulling her close to his side. When she shifted away, he tightened his grip and gave her a look that seemed very recognizable to Amber. *Pure Daddy.*

"I just took a job at General Hospital," Amber admitted.

"Not me. I'm still in the think tank in DC," Maisie shared. "And I don't think they're letting you out of Nashville, Colt."

"Coming home sounds good now," he said, looking at Harper before drawing her in for another kiss.

Amber waited until Miranda drifted away before asking, "Have I missed something?"

Harper opened her mouth to answer but stopped abruptly. Colt stepped in smoothly. "Congratulate us. Harper finally agreed to be my girl."

"Wow! I'm so happy for you. Why didn't you say something?" Amber asked.

"We needed this to be secret for a while. Now, we're ready to tell the world," Colt answered, and Harper nodded with a shy smile.

"Rio sent this and said he's got your favorite song keyed up. Come sing for us," a cute waitress chirped, holding out two microphones.

"Oh, I…" Harper tried to say no but Colt steered her to the small stage.

Amber heard his, "Do this for me, Angel. I've wanted to sing with you for more than seven thousand days…" before his voice drifted away.

"Did you know?" Maisie asked, tugging on Amber's elbow as she scrutinized Beau's face as well.

"I didn't have a clue."

"Neither did I," Beau swore, holding up a hand.

CHAPTER 6

The quieter classmates drifted away from Murphy's around ten o'clock, leaving the party crowd in high gear. Amber said goodbye to Beau and Maisie as they left. Harper and Colt disappeared mysteriously without telling anyone they were heading out.

I should go home, Amber thought before remembering the house would be empty with her folks on their cruise. She wasn't quite ready for that.

Automatically, she searched for Rio and spotted him at his usual spot behind the bar. *Damn, he looks good.* Rio had been handsome when he was thirty-one, but he was all silver fox gorgeous now.

Rio's hair was longer on top and flopped over his brow as he shook the drink shaker. His form-fitting T-shirt outlined the muscles in his chiseled torso, making her fingers ache to touch him. Amber clenched her thighs together as her body reacted to the mere sight of him.

As if he'd felt Amber watching him, Rio looked up. Without breaking eye contact, he poured the drink into the fancy martini glass and set it in front of the chattering woman. Amber saw the customer follow his line of vision to see her, and saw her bristle as he walked away from the bar.

Amber watched him stalk forward, focused completely on her. The crowd must have sensed something, for the last of the partiers moved out of his way to create an open pathway to her side. Time between them evaporated as his eyes held her gaze captive.

When he stopped in front of her, Amber watched his mouth move and read his whispered, "Little girl," on his lips. His hand reached out to smooth a strand of her hair back from her face, and she recognized her name in a heart inked into his palm. A strangled sound burst from her lips as she crossed the last few inches that separated them to press herself against his hard chest.

"Rio," she sighed as she brazenly lifted her lips to ask for a kiss she'd always dreamed about.

He stroked his fingers through her fiery hair to cradle her skull. "I'm not going to disappear this time, Amber. You're all grown up, Little girl."

"This doesn't have to be serious, Rio. Just kiss me."

"I didn't come back to have a fling, Amber. We'll take it slow until you're ready for all that I will ask of you. Come. Sit and talk to me," Rio commanded softly before leaning forward to press a kiss on her forehead.

As he stepped away, Rio slid his fingers down her arm, setting all the nerves in his path on fire. "Come," he repeated, taking her hand and squeezing it gently.

Amber trailed him to the bar. Customers filled all the chairs as she approached, and Amber hesitated, not knowing where to go. Rio nodded at her, and she knew he'd take care of it as they paused by a familiar stool.

When Rio slid behind the bar, he pulled a cold draft and set it in front of the young man in the seat Rio had always reserved for Amber. "Joel, that pretty blonde over there just bought you a beer. You should go thank her."

"Really? The one in the red dress?"

"That's her. Her name is Tracy. Go introduce yourself," Rio directed.

Quickly, Joel slid from the stool and rounded the bar. Amber laughed and took his place. She crossed her legs and leaned against the bar. "Is that going to go well?" she asked, nodding at the man now chatting with the infamous woman in red.

"They needed an introduction, and we needed a stool. Now they can see if there's more than a physical attraction. The two have been checking each other out all evening," Rio assured her.

"And we get to see if there's more than a physical attraction, too?" Amber teased. She liked that the hubbub of the bar created a private space for them to talk without others listening.

"Oh, there's that, definitely. But we don't need an introduction. Let's see if I remember everything. Your favorite color is green. You hate the nickname Sparky. You'd rather be Amberella, or Ella for short. You love peanuts in the shell and hate cashews. You always wanted to play football instead of being a cheerleader, and you consider your biggest flaw to be your size-nine feet."

Amber looked at him in shock. "You remember all that about me?"

"I do. I'd have to disagree with you about your feet. You're killing me in those shoes."

Amber followed his glance over her crossed thighs and down her snug jeans to the high-heeled shoes she'd bought just for the reunion. No nurse would ever wear those regularly. She extended one shoe out to consider the heel.

"They're killers," she agreed playfully. "I'll take them off as soon as possible."

"What can I get you?" Rio asked.

"How about a strawberry daiquiri with some rum this time?"

"I don't want you to have an excuse for anything you choose to do," Rio stated firmly.

"I'm a big girl, Rio. I'm not going to do anything I don't want to do," she assured him.

She thought about that brave statement as he crafted a drink with a splash of alcohol and set it in front of her. Gathering her courage, she decided not to waste any time and asked, "Rio, what do you want from me?"

"Everything. The last time I saw you wasn't the right time. You needed to spread your wings and I needed to wait until you were ready for all that I would demand."

"Demand?" she echoed, leaning closer.

"Rio, I need three IPAs, a scotch on the rocks, and four strawberry daiquiris," one of the waitresses called from the service bar. "Have the reunion ladies worn out the blender yet?"

"Not yet. On it, Jeri," Rio called back as he moved smoothly to create the drinks.

Seeing Amber chuckle, the server summed her up as one of the celebrants. "Sorry."

"No problem. I'm Amber Murphy. I understand bar trends," Amber reassured her. She'd sat in this very spot too many times and watched one order blossom into a dozen as people coveted what someone else was drinking.

"Oh. Sorry. I haven't met you before. I'm Jeri," the cheerful waitress introduced herself, appearing to realize she was talking to the former owner's daughter. "I've been here a bit over a month. I worked with your dad for three days before Rio took over."

"Really? Rio's owned Murphy's for a month?" Amber mused before seeing the confusion on the server's face. "Sorry, just thinking aloud. I'm glad to meet you, Jeri."

That smile froze on Amber's face as Jeri reached over the bar to grab unnecessary lime wedges for the margaritas as Rio set them on her tray. The motion seemed deliberate, as if to draw Rio's attention to the low-cut Murphy's T-shirt Jeri wore.

Amber's gaze flashed to meet Rio's as possessive anger flared inside her stomach at the young server's obvious attempt to flirt. His serious expression calmed her slightly.

"Jeri, Amber is my person." Rio claimed her easily and established a boundary.

"Oh! Sorry." Without a second thought, Jeri was off to deliver her drinks.

"You'll have to trust me," Rio said in a low voice. "My interests are more focused than a random encounter."

"I hadn't ever thought about the temptation here. Maybe I'm just a momentary challenge."

"Take a second to replay our relationship," Rio suggested.

"Do we have a relationship?" Amber answered flippantly.

When Rio simply looked at her before busying himself with the next drink order, Amber considered what he'd suggested. She'd known Rio during her tumultuous teen years. He'd always been glad to see and talk with her.

"Why did it take you so long to come back?" she asked.

"You needed time to become your own person. I was too old for you then."

"You're still thirteen years older than I am," she reminded Rio.

"You're a highly skilled nurse who's traveled the world now. You know who you are and what you want out of life."

"I knew what I wanted then, too," she reminded him.

He nodded, acknowledging her feelings. She liked that he didn't try to discount those. Rio had always listened to her.

"Perhaps it was me that needed to grow up, Amberella," he suggested.

The nickname made her smile. He'd always been the only one to call her that. "Are you grown up now?"

"Yes."

She could question that succinct answer or she could just accept it. Amber considered the time they'd lost after Rio disappeared. Were there any experiences she'd want erased from her life after going to college? Mentally shaking her head, Amber acknowledged there weren't. She was happy with herself and ready to settle down.

"Would you like to spend the day with me tomorrow?" Rio asked, startling her from her thoughts.

"Yes," she answered, mirroring his answer and making him laugh. Her gaze devoured his appearance as he enjoyed their interaction.

Rio's head tilted back, and his hand pressed to his chest as mirth welled from inside him. She loved the crinkle of the laugh wrinkles at the corners of his eyes. He'd always enjoyed life and made anything fun. Amber had missed that in her life.

"I'm glad you came back, Rio."

"I'm glad we're both here."

Abandoning the drink order, Rio rounded the bar and held out a hand to tug her from the stool. "It's late. You've had a long drive. Are you okay to drive?"

"Someone kept the alcohol light in my drinks tonight."

"I'll pick you up at nine for breakfast. Give me your phone," he requested.

Fumbling through her purse, she located the device and unlocked the screen for him. Rio added himself to her contacts and then called his phone. She liked that he took care of everything. Rio made things easy.

"Let me walk you out to your car," he suggested as he wrapped a powerful arm around her waist.

Automatically, Amber sucked in her tummy.

"Be yourself, Ella. I don't want you to be anything else," he urged as he ushered her out the door.

When they reached her car, Rio crowded her against the flashy purple sports car. "Got your fancy wheels, huh?"

Amber forgot to answer as he lowered his lips to taste hers. Pressing slow, deep kisses to her lips, Rio didn't rush her. She curled her fingers into the hard flesh of his waistline, savoring the feel of his weight pinning her to the paint.

"Go home, Little girl. I'll be there at nine. Wear these jeans—different shoes. We'll take my bike," Rio told her as he stepped back to open her door.

Driving from the parking lot, Amber watched him disappear from her view. *Damn.* She missed him already.

CHAPTER 7

Waking up the next morning in the quiet house was a bit surreal. Her old room was now her mother's library, so she was in the guest room on the far side of the house. It felt a bit like she was an interloper—especially since her parents weren't home.

Amber grabbed her phone to check the time and relaxed against the pillows. She had an hour before Rio would get there. Reflecting back on her feelings when she'd seen him, Amber knew her heart had never lurched inside her chest at the sight of anyone like it had last night.

She'd loved her time traveling to different cities and hospitals, but Rio had always hovered in the back of her mind. Amber could only laugh at the number of times she had turned around, sure that the man she'd seen out of the corner of her eye was Rio. It never had been except for last night.

Forcing herself out of bed, she showered quickly and pulled on jeans and a T-shirt. She had packed light as she always did. Hopefully, being casual would be okay with Rio. She'd only brought one cocktail dress for the fancy reunion dinner that night.

Amber shook her head at herself. *It's breakfast! Rio won't expect me to be wearing pearls and high heels. He already warned me about the stilettos.*

Laughing, Amber paid special attention to putting on her makeup. She wanted to look good for Rio. Smoothing out a few lines and wrinkles, Amber didn't usually take time to study the changes that had come with time. She definitely wasn't the same cheerleader she'd been in high school.

When she was ready, Amber let herself out the front door and sat on the steps. Rio had dropped off keys to her dad back in high school, so she expected he'd remember where her parents' house was located.

A rumble of motorcycle pipes caught her attention. Looking up, she spotted Rio as he turned the corner into the cul-de-sac—and stopped breathing. *Holy Fuck!* She felt her panties get wet as arousal flooded her body. As a nurse, she'd seen a lot of serious motorcycle accident injuries. Watching Rio approach, she could understand why women were drawn to the risk-takers.

Rio on a bike was like rich chocolate coating an ice cream bar. He was drool worthy. Sitting casually on the seat, it was obvious Rio had driven a motorcycle a few thousand times before. His powerful thighs straddled the machine, and his muscular arms held it under control. Quickly, she lifted her phone and took a picture.

It was dangling in her hand when his helmet turned to look toward her location. One hand lifted from the handlebars to wave.

Amber stood as he turned into the driveway. Walking slowly to the mechanical beast, she waited for him to take his helmet off. Rio cradled it under one arm and brushed his hair back with his free hand.

"I hoped you'd be brave and come for a ride with me. We can take your car if you'd rather," he suggested.

"I've never ridden on a bike. As I remember, you'd never take me for a ride when I was a kid. Are you a safe driver?" she questioned, trying to convince herself she wasn't getting on behind him regardless of how he answered.

"Your folks would have never allowed that. And now? I'd never risk such precious cargo. Want to live on the wild side?"

She nodded before she realized what she was doing.

"Good girl." With a flick of his fingers, Rio turned off the engine.

After pressing the kickstand into place, he swung one leg over the bike and set his helmet on the seat before unbuckling one of the saddlebags. "I have an extra helmet I carry in case I have a passenger."

Instant jealousy flared through her. "I'm not one of your floozies, Rio."

He whirled around to pace toward her. Stopping in front of her, Rio hooked his fingers into his front pockets. "I didn't plan to talk about this here. But let's get it out in the open. Have you been celibate since you left for college?"

"It's been twenty years since I saw you last. I didn't think I would ever see you again," Amber answered in shock.

"I'll take that as a no. I also didn't think fate would bring us together again. Did I screw a never-ending parade of other women? No. I kept looking for someone special to pretend was you. Anyone I found wasn't... You."

She swallowed hard.

"Do you have any questions you need me to answer before breakfast?" he asked quietly.

"No. I'm sorry. I jumped to conclusions."

He nodded, accepting her apology as he unbuckled the chin strap. "Let me try this again. Back in Kansas City, my two-hundred-pound *male* buddy usually bummed a ride home after work. This helmet might be a bit big, but it will work for today."

"Oh! Okay," she nodded, appalled at how wrong she had been. Amber reached for the helmet and tugged it into place.

Rio brushed her hands away and fastened the strap himself. Tugging experimentally, he nodded. "It's not a bad fit. I always thought Eric had a little head on that enormous body."

A snort of laughter escaped from her lips at the image of some hulking guy with a teeny head. His dancing eyes revealed he had enjoyed her unladylike gust of amusement. "Take me to breakfast. I'm obviously growing faint with hunger."

"As you wish, Little girl." He flipped her face shield into place.

"Are we going to talk about that?" she asked, referring to his endearment.

"Yes. Let me get on the bike to stabilize it before you climb on." Rio moved with ease to flick down a small metal post on each side of the bike before straddling the bike and moving the kickstand out of the way.

Shifting forward a bit on the seat to give her extra room, he instructed, "Swing your foot over the seat and slide into place."

"That sounds so much easier than this looks," she answered, intimidated. Lifting one foot, Amber awkwardly followed his directions and clumsily ended up cozied up to his butt on the seat.

"Oh, sorry. I'm crowding you," she apologized.

"There's only so much room here, Ella. You're going to be closer to me in a minute. Don't worry. I'll enjoy it," he assured her, looking over his shoulder to grin at her.

That devastating smile made the heat inside her flare hotter. Amber nodded. What else could she do?

"Safety, Little girl. Don't move your legs backward. The pipes behind you are hot and will burn your legs, even in those jeans."

Rio paused to pull on his helmet and fasten the buckle. "Hold on to me," he called over his shoulder as he started the motor.

Vibration roared to life between her legs. Amber could feel the throb of the motor. Remembering his words, she wrapped her hands gently around his waist.

"Hold on, Amberella." Rio tugged her arms around his body until she hugged him tightly. "That's it. We move as one unit. When I lean, you lean with me. We won't tip over—the momentum keeps us up. Can you find the foot pegs?"

"Foot pegs?" she echoed and lifted her feet onto the metal supports she remembered him lowering. "Oh! Got it."

"Hold on. Here we go." Rio carefully backed the bike into the street and eased the machine forward.

Grabbing hold of his T-shirt as they rolled forward, Amber tried to pretend she didn't feel the taut muscles under the thin cotton. A few twitching curtains in the neighbors' windows told her she'd hear from her parents when those living close by reported her activities. Amber pushed that idea out of her mind. She was past the age when her mom and dad could tell her how to live her life—well, past the time she had to listen to them.

"You'd listen to your Daddy," a little voice told her.

Amber was pleased to have the distraction of stopping for the first time on the bike. She held her breath at the neighborhood entrance as Rio braked and her pelvis scooted forward on the leather seat. Immediately, she tried to wiggle backward to put some distance between them. His hand clamped over her thigh, stopping her movement as the bike moved underneath them.

"Shift as you need to while we're moving. When we're still, your motion can throw off our balance if I'm not anticipating it," he called over his shoulder. "You're doing great. Just relax. I've got you."

"Sorry."

He patted her thigh before placing his hand back on the grips and turning into an opening in the traffic. She remembered to lean with him even though it felt like they'd topple over.

"Good girl," drifted back to her, and she grinned over his shoulder and tried to relax. His approval shouldn't mean so much, but it did.

Amber quickly gave up her attempts to maintain even a slight distance between their bodies. She hugged Rio tight and enjoyed the excuse to be close to him. Between the vibration under her and his heat and scent filling her senses, Amber's mind was on overload. She did the only thing she could and abandoned herself completely to the experience.

Before she knew it, Rio turned into a parking lot at a new diner she'd never tried. She stayed perfectly still until he pulled to a stop and dropped his feet to brace the bike.

"You did great, Ella," he cheered, turning back to look at her.

"I recovered from my terror," she joked as she tried to dismount gracefully. Her movements were a bit choppy, but she didn't tumble to the ground.

"Were you terrified?" he asked. "I could only see you smiling."

"You could see me?" she squeaked, flipping her face plate up.

Rio pointed to his side-view mirrors. "I can catch glimpses of you as we ride."

"That's embarrassing."

"Not at all. You were having a great time. That's what I wanted to see. If you'd been terrified, I would have returned to your house to take your car," he shared, stepping off the bike with the ease of someone who'd done it a million times.

"It was fun. I liked it." Amber squeezed her inner thighs together, still feeling an echo of the vibration she'd enjoyed intimately. He didn't have to know how much she enjoyed it.

"Good. Let's go have some breakfast." Rio helped her take her helmet off before stripping his off as well.

With both stored in the saddlebags, Rio took her hand. Amber tried to be cool. When his hand squeezed hers, she peeked up at him.

"I'm glad you're home," he told her softly.

That simple statement went straight to her heart. A question popped into her brain. What if she hadn't come home for the reunion? She'd missed her friends, but she hadn't known he was waiting.

CHAPTER 8

Rolling that thought over in her head, Amber allowed him to guide her into the diner. As they followed the server to their table, she was aware of the number of admiring looks that followed Rio—both female and male. She didn't blame them. Staring at such a handsome man was natural. Much to her surprise, it made her feel jealous.

When they reached a far booth, the server set their menus on the table and waved them into seats. Amber slid onto one of the bench seats. "Oh," she said in surprise as he joined her on the same side. Quickly, Amber scooted over as Rio settled next to her.

Busying herself by looking at the menu, Amber couldn't stop the question that burst from her lips. "What if I'd never come back here?"

"Then I would have come to find you. That's actually how I reconnected with your father. I visited Murphy's to chat with him about you."

"What would you like to drink?" the server's voice interrupted them.

"Coffee and water, please," Amber requested.

"I'll take the same," Rio echoed, before anticipating the next question. "Cream and sugar for the lady, please."

"Of course. Our special today is cinnamon roll pancakes. You can order one, two, or three," the waitress suggested.

"One for me." Amber accepted the easiest way to order with relief. She wouldn't have to pretend to focus on the menu.

"Chicken and waffles, please," Rio ordered.

When the server departed, he turned back to wrap his arm across the back of the bench seat so he could look at Amber. "Your dad wasn't comfortable telling me your address. He did tell me you were coming back for the reunion."

"And somehow you ended up buying the bar?" she asked, incredulous.

"When your father mentioned you'd be working at the hospital, I mentioned I was interested in starting a small bar and settling down. I think he surprised himself when he offered to sell Murphy's to me."

"And you accepted?"

"I did."

"Just like that?" Amber asked.

Rio paused as the server placed steaming mugs of coffee and ice water in front of them. He lined up four creamers in front of Amber and scooted the sugar container in front of her before picking up his mug and taking a drink.

"I still don't see how you can drink that black. It's so bitter," Amber observed, emptying all the creamers into her cup and adding a healthy amount of sugar. She took a drink and settled back against the padded booth with a sigh of delight. "Perfect."

"Just as you've always liked it," Rio said with a grin.

Taking another sip, she replayed the conversation in her head. "Did you buy the bar because I planned to move back here?"

"I did."

Mind blown, she looked at him, unsure what to say to that. "Why has it taken you so long, Rio? Twenty years was a long time to wait to reconnect."

"You weren't ready at first. Can you imagine not being a nurse and traveling as you have?"

She picked up her coffee cup to give herself a few seconds to think. He deserved for her to tell him the truth.

"I can't. Who knows? Maybe this isn't supposed to work?" she asked, waving her hand back and forth between their bodies.

"Is that what you actually think?" he asked, his brows pulling together.

Amber stared at him as she wrestled with the turmoil inside her. She hadn't ever wanted a relationship with anyone as much as she had with Rio. Finally, she forced herself to be brave.

"No. It's just scary. I've never..." Amber let her voice trail away as she looked around the packed restaurant. No one could possibly hear her over the hubbub inside.

"Never found another Daddy?" he asked.

"Oh, I think I found a few of those in twenty years. I just didn't find the right Daddy."

The smile returned to his face, and Rio relaxed back against the booth. "Good."

"This smells amazing," the server confided as she placed a huge pancake on a plate in front of them. "I'm going to have one on my break."

Amber leaned in to inhale the incredible scent. "Oh, wow! Mmm!" She wiggled in her seat and froze when her leg pressed against Rio's.

His hand dropped to span her thigh, holding her in place against him and squeezing lightly as the server placed his order in front of him. Unable to resist, Amber leaned toward his plate to give it a sniff. The hot fried chicken had a delicious aroma as well.

"Yum. Is that really a good combination?"

"It is. You can try it. First, take a taste of yours," he instructed, removing his hand from her leg to pick up his fork and knife. Instantly, she missed the heat of his touch.

Turning her attention to her plate, Amber cut a piece of the specialty pancake that filled the plate. "This is incredibly large," she pointed out. "I think it's bigger than my head."

"I think you might be right." He watched her take a bite.

"Oh, my goodness! We'll have to come here again. This could be addictive," she mumbled around her bite.

When she had swallowed, Rio handed her his fork, loaded with a small bite of waffle and chicken stacked on each other and dipped into golden syrup. She hesitated to take his fork.

"I just had myself tested two weeks ago. I'm clean. Is there anything that I should know about your health?" Rio asked softly.

Amber stared at him for a few seconds before replying, "What? No!" as she tried to understand what he was sharing and asking. Casting a furtive look around the restaurant, she made sure no one was listening.

"No one is interested in anything other than the deliciousness on their plate. Would you like to try this?" he asked, holding the fork out to her.

Automatically reaching for it this time, Amber accepted the utensil and put the bite in her mouth. Savory, sweet, crunchy sensations captivated her taste buds. "That's the best thing I've ever eaten!"

"Then we share," Rio suggested, taking back his fork.

She saw him notice a dribble of syrup on his hand, deposited most probably when she'd hesitated to accept his fork. Amber couldn't keep herself from staring as he lifted his tattoo-decorated hand to his mouth and licked off the sweet concoction. Clenching her thighs together as fantasies exploded in her mind, she heard Rio groan and her gaze jumped to his suddenly serious face.

"You are going to kill me, baby," he muttered, before adjusting the fly of his jeans and drawing her attention to his growing bulge.

When she focused on his reaction, Rio lifted her chin, dragging her gaze from his crotch. "If you don't want to walk out of here with me fully erect, stop thinking what you're imagining and eat," he growled.

"Oh! Sorry!" Amber cut another bite of her pancake and shoved it into her mouth. As she chewed, the mental image of all the diners watching as they walked through the room blossomed in her mind. Unable to stop, she tried to stifle the laughter that welled inside her.

"Remember this, Little girl, when I take my revenge and keep you on the edge for longer than you wish," he told her softly as he placed a bite of chicken on her cinnamon pancake. "Try that combination. Sample everything that delights you."

Was he saying what she thought he was? Internally, Amber nodded to herself. Nothing would be off limits with Rio. Things she'd never been brave enough to ask for.

Rio nodded and urged, "Try it, Ella. Tell me if you like it."

Amber stabbed the chicken and pancake combination and dabbed it into the syrup. Putting it in her mouth, she chewed. It was good, but not the same.

"Sometimes, an original combination is perfect and can't be improved."

She studied his face. There was no mistaking that his words had more than one meaning. He wasn't just talking about chicken and waffles.

Deciding just to ask rather than wonder, she asked, "Do you think we were perfect?"

"Not then. You needed to experience the world, and I wasn't the man I needed to be. Now, I hope we're as close to perfect for each other as possible."

"So… What does that mean? You want to date? Go to breakfast? Screw around?"

"When we're intimate, it will be because we're ready to make a commitment to each other. You tell me when you're ready to explore all that we can be. Until then, we date and spend time together." He held another bite of chicken and waffle to her lips.

Allowing him to feed her, Amber considered all he summed up tidily. She chewed slowly before swallowing. "Are you going to disappear again?"

"I've put down roots here and hope you will, too."

She wasn't going to allow him to skirt the question. Amber needed to hear him answer clearly and directly. "What does that mean? I need for you to tell me whether you'll leave. I don't want to risk my heart if you decide you need to disappear for my own good."

"The last time I left tore me apart, Ella. All my efforts to do the right thing were decimated by that one decision. I plan to be selfish now and keep you for myself."

Studying his face once again, she nodded. Amber had seen Rio evade many pursuing women by tweaking the truth. His excuses were never complete lies, but not entirely accurate, either. She knew how to read his expressions—or she did twenty years ago.

"Okay. I'll trust you."

"Thank you, Amber."

They ate in silence for a few minutes before Amber noticed a group of ladies a few tables away holding an animated conversation. From time to time, they would turn to look at Rio and then lean in together to whisper furiously.

"I think more people than me are glad you returned to town," she commented wryly.

Rio followed her line of vision and nodded at the group, who called their good mornings. His attention refocused on Amber. "What shall we do today? You have a reunion dinner and dance tonight," he recalled.

"I do. I don't suppose you could go with me?"

"Thank you. I'd love to be your escort," Rio accepted instantly.

"Can you be gone from the bar?"

"The bar is my investment. There are many competent bartenders who are pleased to have the hours and the tips. My priority is always going to be you."

"You didn't have to be there last night?" she asked.

"Not to work. I did need to be there to see if the spark that linked us together still glowed brightly."

"You were a much bigger surprise than Colt showing up, acting like he was Harper's date. I need to call her today to find out what's going on."

"Why not sit back and watch what happens? Harper was always one of my favorites of your friends. I'd like to see her live her happiest life."

"Do you think that would be with Colt?"

"Why not?"

"They seem to be so different from each other now. Colt is famous everywhere and Harper is happiest with the children she tends," Amber pointed out.

"Is she?" Rio asked simply, making Amber sit up straighter as she considered his implication. Could Harper be happier?

CHAPTER 9

*R*io had given her a look that stopped her offer to pay half in its tracks. He quickly settled the bill with cash and what looked like a generous tip before sliding out of the booth and holding out a hand to assist her.

Several people greeted them individually and welcomed her or Rio back to town. She knew the gossip mongers were going to have a heyday talking about them.

"So, how many people in there think we just slept together?" Amber asked with a shake of her head.

Rio looked at her and laughed. "If only their fantasies were true. There are those that live vicariously through others."

"You don't?"

"I don't. I like people but that's where it ends. Their lives are theirs to enjoy or not. I plan to make the most of mine now. Do you have any plans for the day?"

"Not really. I'll make sure the wrinkles in my dress have fallen out and maybe redo my nails."

"Do you have any plans with your friends?"

"No. Maisie, Colt, and Beau are spending time with their families,

I'm sure. Harper probably has a daycare full of babies and toddlers even though it's Saturday."

"Then, you're all mine."

"O-okay." Amber liked the sound of that way too much.

A few minutes later, Rio started his motorcycle and pulled out of the parking lot with Amber safely helmeted behind him. She tried to hold herself slightly away from his body to give herself a buffer from his appeal.

Rio steered the motorcycle through town and turned down a country lane. She hadn't driven down this road since graduation. It led to the gathering and party spot all high schoolers back in her day knew. It looked different now. Someone had removed all the concealing brush, and there were actual streetlights scattered along the length of the road.

She bet high schoolers now had a different area to escape from everyone's view. This was too open and accessible. Someone must have bought the land from old man Howard. Maybe his kids had decided to settle down here.

She looked around, seeing it through fresh eyes. Before, her concentration had focused on the other teenagers packed with her in the vehicle. Now in the late morning, it had transformed into an awe-inspiring view. The trees formed an arch over the pavement and the leaves filtered the sunshine, lowering the temperature. Amber huddled closer to Rio's frame as she enjoyed the beauty of nature around her.

"Are you okay?" Rio asked, glancing over his shoulder.

"I'm great. Just taking advantage of your heat," she answered with a laugh.

Rio reached one arm back to wrap around her waist and pulled her effortlessly against his body, erasing the smidgen of space she'd tried to leave between them. Amber tightened her arms around his waist and relaxed, giving up any attempt to resist his allure.

"That's it, Ella. Leave everything to me."

She liked the feeling of not being responsible. Nursing required being alert at all times. People's lives depended on her skill. Holding on to a handsome man in this beautiful place felt amazing. The fresh air streamed around them as the powerful motor swept them away from civilization. She loved the feeling of freedom that came from riding with him.

"Thank you for bringing me here, Rio," she shouted against the wind.

Instead of answering verbally, he wrapped one powerful hand around her thigh and squeezed.

Rio slowed and turned off a side road. Amber missed his hand immediately when he'd returned it to the handlebars. A few minutes later, he pulled into a small alcove and parked. Amber stood, swung her leg over the seat, and watched Rio turn off the bike before joining her. She wondered if she'd ever tire of watching the play of his muscles as he dismounted.

"That was lovely," she breathed when he was by her side.

"Just wait." Rio took her hand. "Are you okay to walk a bit?"

"After that breakfast, I need to walk for miles," she bemoaned, patting her hip. Her job was active, and Amber was strong, but she definitely wasn't in the same slim teenage shape she'd been in as a cheerleader in high school.

"You are perfect," Rio assured her. Dropping Amber's hand, he smoothed his hand over her back to cup her bottom before repeating himself. "Perfect."

"I'm afraid you're going to be disappointed," Amber blurted.

"Never."

His simple answer made her stop. Before she could argue with him, Rio pulled her close and kissed her deeply. Her worries dissipated as she clung to his snug T-shirt, rising on her toes to press her mouth fully to his.

They were both breathing heavily when his lips lifted from hers. Amber stared into his deep brown eyes. The warmth inside them reassured her it was okay to take this risk.

"Is it our time now?" she whispered.

"Finally," he breathed.

Rio turned back to his bike and unfastened a saddlebag to pull out what looked like a vintage quilt. He slung it over one arm before holding a hand to her. "Come with me."

With their fingers linked, they walked along quietly, listening to the birds and the rustle of leaves. She halted when their walk led to the bank of a small, picturesque creek. The sound of the crystal-clear water splashing delighted her. Amber stared around at the beautiful spot.

"Wow! It's gorgeous here."

Glancing up at the banks, she admired the green space and the beautiful trees that led up a gentle slope. "Can we go up there? I want to see what everything looks like from that vantage point."

"Of course." Rio handed her the blanket before scooping her up in his arms and wading across the shallow water.

"Wait! I can walk," she protested.

"My boots will keep my feet dry," he assured her and set her feet back on the ground on the other side.

"Sorry. I didn't mean for you to have to carry me," she apologized.

"Little girls need to learn that Daddies have their own way of caring for those they love. You also have to trust me," he stressed, taking the blanket back from her.

"I'm not used to someone being in my life... You know, with that big of a presence," she tried to explain.

"Is it unpleasant?" he probed, watching her expressions.

Amber paused to think for a fraction of a second. "No. It feels good. It just isn't what I'm used to," she explained.

"Time will take care of that," he said and smiled at her. Rio reached out a hand to gently tuck a few strands of hair from her face. "Damn, I'm glad we have another chance together now. Let's make the most of it."

Nodding, Amber stepped forward to hug him tightly. "I think that's a very good idea."

"Let's go up and look from your spot," he suggested, kissing the top of her head as he squeezed her to his hard frame.

"I bet it's unbelievable there," she predicted.

Every few minutes, she turned around to look down the hill to check if they were in the best spot yet. Just below the highest point of the rise, Amber knew she had found the place.

"Here, Rio. I think this is best."

"Let's try it out," he suggested and spread out the blanket.

"Oh, I know this pattern. My grandmother had one on her bed. It's a wedding ring quilt. How did you get this?"

"A neighbor gave it to me a few years ago. Her kids didn't want it and she couldn't stand for it to go to a landfill or be torn apart for rags. Tessa made the quilt for her wedding and used it every day for seventy years until her husband passed away."

"Oh, we shouldn't put it on the ground then. It's a collector's item," Amber said, leaning down to pick it up.

Rio stopped her by capturing her hands and holding them. He looked deep in her eyes and said, "It's okay, baby. Tessa would only give it to me if I promised to use it. She knew it wouldn't last forever and wanted someone else to have happy memories because of it."

"Oh," Amber said and felt tears well into her eyes.

"Tessa is gone now?" she guessed. Even after all these years of being a nurse, she felt the passing of others.

"She is. Died in her sleep the next night. She didn't have to go to the nursing home that was the next step for her. Tessa already told me she was ready to rejoin her husband whenever her time came," Rio shared before squeezing Amber's hands to comfort her.

"So, we use the quilt. We enjoy it and if it's still around when our adventures are done and still has more life in the fabric, we pass it on," he stated firmly.

Without another word, Amber toed off her shoes and stepped onto the soft material. Sitting, she leaned over to unlace Rio's boots in a wordless request.

"Okay, Ella. We'll do it your way," he allowed, leaving his boots on the grass and stepping onto the material in his bright crimson socks.

"Red?" she asked, feeling herself smirk. He didn't seem like a man who would wear red socks.

"All my socks are red."

"Really? Just your personal flair?"

"A subtle reminder to myself of what I was missing," he answered, reaching down to tug on her still vibrant auburn hair.

She stared at him without knowing what to say as her heart skipped a beat inside her chest. Amber clasped her hands together and pressed them against her breastbone as her emotions whirled inside her. Surely that couldn't be true, yet somehow, she knew it was.

As she thought about his revelation, Rio settled behind her and effortlessly lifted Amber to sit with her back against his chest within the circle of his legs. He pressed a kiss against her hair before wrapping his arms around her torso to hold her close.

"What do you think?" he asked, waving a hand across the vista before them.

Staring off into the beauty that unfurled in front of their gaze, Amber leaned back against the rock-hard strength that supported her. "Oh, Rio. It's gorgeous. I'd give up coffee to see this view every morning. No, that's a lie. I'd want a cup of coffee to enjoy as I sit and devour this view."

Rio laughed softly against her ear. The deep sound sent shivers down her spine. *Is there anything about him that isn't pure male hotness?*

His arms hugged her tight before relaxing slightly. "I thought I'd searched every inch of this property looking for the perfect site to build my house, but this is a better location than anything I've discovered. Leave it to you to find it for us."

"For us?" Amber picked up on that last statement and twisted in his arms to look at him.

"For us, Ella. I bought this land before I picked up the bar. I don't want to share it with anyone else. This will be a perfect home for us. Close enough to town that you can get to the hospital easily even in bad weather, and enough empty space around us that we can live our lives the way we want to."

"We're really going to do this?" she whispered.

"Yes."

Amber scrambled to turn around. She needed to see his expressions. When she settled into position facing him, his hands stroked reassuringly down her arms. "What if we don't…" She searched her mind for the right word to use. "What if we don't mesh well together?"

CHAPTER 10

*R*io wrapped his hands around her waist and pulled her to straddle his pelvis. Her legs extended over his thighs. He lifted one hand to cup her face and pressed a soft kiss against her lips before groaning and deepening their exchange.

Clinging to him, Amber answered his passionate kisses as she stroked his shoulders and back. Needing more, she daringly grabbed the waistband of his T-shirt and pulled it over his wind-tousled hair. Instantly, Rio lifted his arms to allow her to remove it completely.

Amber froze as she looked over his ripped body. Years of fitness and activity had honed his muscles into a work of art. Unable to resist, she traced the grooves in his torso leading down to where they disappeared under his waistband. Subconsciously, she licked her lips, wanting to taste his sun-kissed skin.

"You're killing me, Little girl," he groaned and tugged away the garment she clutched in her hands to toss it to the edge of the quilt.

"My turn," he told her in a low growly tone that pushed her arousal higher. His hands slid under the back of her T-shirt and pulled it up over her head, revealing her plain cotton bra.

"I wasn't expecting to vamp anyone this weekend," she whispered, sorry she wasn't wearing something lacy and daring for him.

Rio traced the swell of her breasts pressed against the edges of her bra. "Beautiful, Ella. You don't need to wear anything fancy for me. I vote we take this off."

He trailed his fingers along the band of the garment to the hooks behind her and deftly unfastened them. Rio leaned down to kiss her as his hands swept the bra straps over her arms. As he teased her lips with soft kisses, he cupped her breasts. When he brushed his work-roughened thumbs over her nipples, Amber's breath caught in her chest.

When he kissed down the length of her neck, Amber arched her head to the side, presenting herself to those nibbling, caressing lips. He seemed to know exactly where to touch her as he explored her body slowly. When Rio reached the treasures he fondled, he raised his head to look down at her.

"Damn, Ella. You're captivating. I need to taste you."

She gasped as he whirled their position around to stretch her out on the quilt beneath them. Reclining at her side, Rio captured one taut tip and pulled it into the heat of his mouth. He lashed his tongue over it as he sucked gently.

Amber threaded her fingers through his silver-flecked hair and held him to her body. When he released the first peak to lavish the same care onto the other, she arched her back to offer her breasts fully to him. His groan of desire fueled the arousal that had built inside her at the first sight of him on his motorcycle.

"Rio, please," she pleaded.

He stroked a hand down her abdomen and glided it under the waistband of her jeans. Covering her cotton panties, Rio explored her heat. He traced the cleft of her pussy and lingered in the wetness that soaked them.

"Ella. I need to be here. Are you ready to be with me?"

"Yes, Rio," she whispered, reaching to unbutton her jeans.

"I'm in charge, baby," he corrected her sternly, withdrawing his hand to brush hers away. He raised her hands above her head and held them securely in one hand before returning his attention to unfastening her pants.

When she struggled against him, Rio paused and met her gaze with his. He said nothing, simply watched her. Searching his face, she could see, written over the passion carved into his features, an unyielding resolve. She would have to give him everything. Rio would never settle for less.

"Rio." She breathed out his name. "I want to touch you."

"I know, Little girl. You'll earn my permission."

Thoughts whirled in her mind as her arousal grew. Her body knew before she could understand. She needed this. Amber wanted him to be in charge.

"Okay, Daddy," she whispered tentatively.

His heat-filled stare made her smile to herself before he pounced. Rio's mouth captured hers. Tangling his tongue with hers, the captivating man seduced her with his dominance. She forced herself to relax her arms, relinquishing control to him.

"You are wearing too many clothes, Ella," he growled against her lips before propping himself up on an elbow. "Keep your hands here."

Rio placed a handful of the soft material against her fingers and tucked it against her palms. Immediately, she gripped the quilt to help her follow his directions. He rewarded her with a hard kiss.

Shifting to kneel at her feet, Rio leaned over her to tug her jeans and panties down her thighs. Amber watched his face as he uncovered her body. The desire etched on his face thrilled her. No man had ever looked at her like this.

When the material cleared her feet, Rio rose to stand at the end of the quilt. His fingers roughly opened his belt and jeans, drawing her attention to the obviously thick shaft that tented the front of his pants. As his zipper lowered, Rio's heavy erection wrapped in cotton jutted forward. Rio stroked down his cock as he looked over her nude body.

"Please," she begged, trying to hurry him up.

"Oh, I'm going to savor you, Ella. I've waited too long to rush."

Her eyes widened and she felt herself nod in response. As Rio pushed his jeans and tight black boxers down, she couldn't figure out where to look. Devouring him with her gaze, she memorized the play of his muscles as he revealed himself to her. She felt her mouth form an O of astonishment as his cock sprang free.

"It will fit, Amberella. I'll make sure of that. Keep those hands where they are," he warned as she reached one lower to stroke herself.

Her face flamed with embarrassment at her automatic move to caress herself. His next words made her look up at his face. "I can't wait to watch you make yourself come, but today, your pleasure belongs to me."

Again, she nodded her agreement before she realized what she was doing. His words seemed to register in her mind in a deeper place, making her follow his directions without conscious thought.

As he stalked forward to drop onto his knees next to her, Amber traced his muscular form with her gaze. Rio loomed over her to kiss her before stroking his hands down her torso. Lingering to tug gently at her nipples, he explored the soft skin covering her ribcage and abdomen.

"Spread your legs."

She shifted her thighs slightly apart and then further when he simply looked at her with a single raised eyebrow. He trailed his fingertips over her mound and traced the cleft of her pussy on her bare skin, just as he had over her cotton panties. Amber parted her legs more, inviting a more intimate touch.

Rio brushed a hand over her inner thigh, making her tilt her hips up toward that caress. He moved over her, settling between her outstretched limbs, and reached below her to cup her bottom. Without warning, he lifted her pelvis to his mouth. His kisses there made her dig her fingers into the quilt as pleasure built inside her.

Exploring her pink folds, Rio hummed his approval of her taste. The vibration spread through her as her body rewarded his caresses with slick juices she could see glistening, not only on her skin, but on his.

Amber moaned and closed her eyes when his tongue traced her opening and dipped inside to explore. It teased over her clit, making her breath catch inside her as he pushed her arousal higher. Tiny nibbles here and there made her try holding her breath in the hope that he'd allow her to climax.

"Come, baby," he commanded, and sucked hard on that small bundle of nerves.

An orgasm crashed over her, shaking her body with the intensity as he lifted his head. She loved that he watched her. His expression told Amber that he enjoyed her pleasure as much as he did his own.

As her body quieted, Rio grabbed a small packet from the pocket of his discarded jeans and quickly donned the protection without complaint or question. Something warm kindled inside her as she realized he wanted to take care of her in all ways.

Impishly, she raised her hands from the ground, still clutching the quilt, holding her arms out to beckon him forward. Rio shook his head and crawled over her body to cage her underneath him, forcing her arms to yield the space. Amber lowered the quilt back to the ground to assume the position he'd placed her in and waited for his next move.

"That's better, Ella. I think you deserve a reward, don't you?" he asked, pressing her thighs widely apart as he pressed two fingers slowly inside her. "This is where I've dreamed of being for twenty years, Amber."

His fingers scissored inside her, preparing her tight channel. He flicked over her most sensitive places, keeping her on edge. Rio lowered his lips to her ear and whispered, "I'm going to fill you, Amber. Are you going to be a good girl for me?"

"Yes!" she shouted into the air, already on the edge of a looming climax.

When he removed his probing fingers, Amber raised her pelvis to chase them and bumped into his thick shaft. Daringly, she rubbed her mound against him, loving his quick intake of breath.

Rio drew back and pressed his cock to her entrance before moving slowly inside. "Breathe, Ella. Relax your muscles for me," he instructed as he stretched her as gently as possible.

The slight burn as he eased inside her added to her desire. She loved the hint of pain that accompanied his complete possession. He seemed to fill all the space inside her body.

When his pelvis finally met hers, Rio captured her gaze. "Good?" he asked, concern obvious even through the passion etched on his features.

"Move. Please."

Rio withdrew and thrust firmly inside her body without stopping. He paused for a few seconds before stroking down her torso to flick her clit. As her muscles tightened around him, he stroked even deeper.

"Touch me, Ella."

Releasing the material from her death grip, Amber lowered her arms to caress his arms and back. She loved the feel of his skin under her fingertips. Daringly, she reached lower to cup one powerful buttock, feeling the shift of his muscles as he thrust inside her. Rio captured her lips and kissed her deeply. She trailed her fingers over his spine to thread her fingers through his thick hair.

As they moved against each other, the beautiful breeze wrapped around them, caressing their skin. Amber blocked the sound of the birds singing to concentrate on the sensations building inside her. She could only focus on Rio and the pleasure he lavished on her.

Arching to meet his next thrust, bliss exploded through her. Rio moaned into her ear as she contracted around him. "Damn, Ella. You feel so good."

He brushed the hair from her face and dropped a line of kisses across her collarbones as he extended the feeling coursing through her with gentle strokes.

When she'd recovered slightly, Rio told her, "One more time, Ella. Come with me this time."

What could she do but nod? Wrapped in his arms, Amber would deny him nothing. She swept her hands down his hard body, searching for those sensitive spots that tantalized him.

Daringly, she wiggled her fingers between their bodies. Touching him as intimately as Rio's increasing thrusts would allow, Amber heard his breath change and felt herself smile. She liked the power of being able to arouse him.

Rio's hands cupped her bottom, raising her body slightly to change the angle of his entrance. Gasping at the feeling, Amber wrapped her free hand around his powerful forearm as she moved to meet his strokes. Unable to delay her climax, she shattered around him.

With a shout that scared birds from their perches, Rio allowed himself to come as he plunged into her, drawing every bit of ecstasy from their bodies. When he finished, Rio rolled to his side and pulled her close to him. After adroitly taking care of the condom, he nestled a heartbeat away from Amber.

She closed her eyes and simply listened to his heartbeat. They were finally together.

CHAPTER 11

When they'd roused to dress, Amber stayed close to the magnetic man who had tantalized her body and mind. She watched him tie his socks around a low-hanging branch of a nearby tree. The bright red of the cotton stood out vividly.

"There. Now I can find this exact spot again. Come look at the house plans," he invited, holding out his hand for hers.

"You've got them here?" she asked, linking her fingers with his.

"No. They're at the condo I've rented."

Intrigued, Amber squeezed his hand. "Let's go."

"That's my girl."

Slowly, they folded up the beautiful quilt and ambled back to the motorcycle, enjoying the intimacy that lingered. She didn't think she'd ever felt closer to anyone. Squeezing his hand, she bumped into his broad shoulder, unable to tell him exactly how she felt.

"Same."

Surprised by his answer, she met his gaze and repeated, "Same?"

"I can't know exactly what's going around in your mind and heart, but I can guarantee that you have rocked my world and I'll never let you go now."

"Okay," she whispered in awe of his openness and commitment to her.

When they reached the motorcycle, Amber stood still as he helped her don the helmet and fasten it into place. Admiring the powerful machine as she waited for him to get ready to leave, she noticed something in the paint. She leaned closer to make out the script letters. ADL.

"Adult dreams for life," she recited, remembering what he'd told her before. He'd had these initials on the battered bike he'd ridden twenty years ago.

"That's not really what it stands for, Amber," he admitted with a rueful smile.

"So, what is ADL really?"

"Amber De Leon."

"Amber... De Leon?"

"I've had that on every bike I've owned, Little girl."

She stared at him wordlessly. Her heart had remained shattered for a long time after she'd headed out of town for college. In the beginning, thoughts of him filled her every waking moment. That had faded over time to frequent memories and a jarring hope at the sight of a stranger in a crowd who looked a bit like Rio. Amber had never forgotten him, either.

Mechanically, she swung her leg over the bike after he settled into place. Emotionally overwhelmed, she welcomed a moment of privacy to wrangle herself under control as they set off to return to town. Amber pressed her cheek against his back and clung to his hard frame.

When Rio covered her hands with one of his, she knew he understood how she felt. Rio had always sensed her feelings. Regardless of any front she put on to fool the world, he got her.

Reaching town, he returned his hand to the handlebar to maneuver safely through the traffic. He drove into a new section of town that Amber had never visited and stopped at a guard shack that controlled the entrance to an exclusive neighborhood.

"Hi, Rio," the older man greeted them as he waved from the small building.

"Hi, Charlie. This is Amber Murphy. She's the other name on my account and will need access."

"Hi, Amber. When you drive in for the first time, I'll get your car make and model with your license plate to complete your registration. Then you can just wave at us as you come in and out."

"Thanks, Charlie," Amber said smoothly, wiggling her fingers against Rio's waist to signal she had questions.

He drove the motorcycle through the quiet neighborhood. Everyone they passed waved hello, and several called Rio's name in greeting. When he pulled into the driveway of decidedly the residence Amber would not call a condo, she scrambled off the bike to look at him with her hands on her hips.

What is going on here?

"Let me put this in the garage and I'll answer all your questions."

Unbuckling her helmet, Amber worked very hard not to tap her foot in annoyance as Rio turned the bike around and backed it into the garage next to a very expensive sports car. She paced forward to return it to him as he stepped off the bike. Within seconds, he wrapped an arm around her waist and steered her inside.

"Are you kidding me? What's going on here, Rio? Did you rob a bank?" she demanded.

"It appears that you made some assumptions about the young man working as a bartender at your dad's establishment," he said with a raised eyebrow. "Come on. Let me get you something to drink. I'm always thirsty after a ride."

"I don't understand this, Rio."

"I know." Opening the refrigerator door, he pulled out a carton of milk and a bottle of chocolate syrup.

As he poured two tall glasses of milk and added syrup to one, Amber collapsed onto one of the kitchen island's barstools.

"I haven't drank chocolate milk since I was twelve," she informed him as he sat it in front of her.

"I bet you still like it."

To prove him wrong, she took a sip. Chocolatey goodness coated her parched throat and settled easily into her churning stomach. "Okay, it's delicious," she admitted and took another drink before waving a hand around in a silent message.

"My family owns the De Leon banks. We don't rob them."

"And you were working in the bar?"

"My father believed all his children needed to find their way in the world. After high school graduation, we received nothing from the family coffers until we were twenty-five and began working for the family."

Amber did some quick math in her head. "You were twenty-five when I was twelve. Why did you stick around at the bar?"

"You were a phenomenal kid. I knew you'd be a remarkable woman. I wanted to watch you grow up."

She stared at him, speechless. He'd made what seemed like a bunch of money to a teenager in tips but looking back now, Amber knew her father had not paid Rio a lot of money. He'd lived in a crappy apartment and ridden a second-hand motorcycle just to stay close to her?

"I also needed to find my niche in the banking business. Your father helped me discover that," he shared.

"My father?"

"He was being swindled by the liquor company he used back then. As I checked in a few deliveries when he was out of the bar, I noted errors in the invoices and reported them. Eventually, he had me check a stack from previous orders. I believe he changed companies after that."

"You could tell something was wrong at a glance?"

"Turns out that's my superpower," he joked.

"That's a pretty handy superpower for a guy whose family is in banking."

"It is," Rio confirmed.

"Are you working two places now?"

"I am. The bar is a hobby. There is a full staff and a couple of managers. I simply keep an eye on the books and bartend when I want to be there."

"And during the day?"

"I'm a forensic accountant—on vacation for a few days currently."

"A forensic accountant?" she echoed.

"Turns out I can look at any list of numbers and see where things don't add up. My family finds that useful," he joked before adding, "And I don't have to wear fancy suits very often."

Amber tried to imagine Rio dressed in anything other than jeans and a T-shirt. "I'd like to see that."

"How about if I wear one tonight to take you to the dinner and dance," he suggested.

"I'd love having you there with me." Amber stared at him, trying to put together all the information she'd learned about him. Her mind whirled with all the revelations and events of the day.

"Drink your milk, Ella. Then I'll put you to bed."

Automatically, she picked up her glass and took another drink. Utter exhaustion dropped over her. Stifling a yawn, she retorted, "I don't take naps."

"You do now."

"I thought we were going to look at the house plans," she reminded him.

"There is plenty of time to review them. Now, it is more important that you rest. Finish your milk."

She picked up her glass and drained it. When Rio approached and offered her his hand, she slid from the stool. Following him through the beautiful, yet livable home, Amber felt at home. It wasn't too fancy that she'd worry about even sitting on the furniture.

Rio stopped at the end of the hall. "Go potty."

As she darted into the bathroom, she saw the master bedroom to the right. When Amber returned to his side, wiping her hands on her jeans to dry them, he pointed out, "There are towels."

"They're too pretty to use."

"No way."

Rio stepped into the bathroom to snag a hand towel from the rack. Taking her hands, he dried them gently before tossing the towel onto the vanity. "Make yourself at home, Little girl."

Steering her to the closed door on the left, he opened the barrier and stood back for her to enter first. Amber walked in to see deep blue walls with a green wavy pattern. A twin four-poster bed sat against the far wall and was draped with gauzy blue-green fabric from the mahogany supports. It felt like she'd just walked under the surface of the sea.

"It's beautiful in here. I would have given my left arm to have a room like this when I was a kid."

"I know."

He guided her gently past an oversized rocker to the side of the bed and tossed the comforter to the bottom of the bed. Kneeling at her feet, Rio slipped her shoes off and set them just under the bed. Smoothly, he rose to his feet and scooped her into his arms to lay her on top of the crisp sheet. Rio spread the soft comforter over her and tucked it around her form.

"Go to sleep. We'll talk when you're rested."

"I can talk now," she mumbled, trying to keep her eyes open. She crossed her arms over her chest, missing Limey. He'd love this room.

"Shhh. I'll stay here until you're asleep, Ella."

Tumbling into dreams, she did not hear him leave.

CHAPTER 12

She woke up in the beautiful room and heard the rattle of pans in the kitchen. Sitting up, she scooted back to sit against the pillows and headboard. A dresser sat across from her with a penguin facing her. It had the cutest expression and a large green bowtie.

"You slept well," Rio said softly from the doorway, making her jump.

"How did you know I was awake?"

"Waddle there showed me when you moved," he explained with a gesture toward the penguin as he walked forward to sit on the edge of the bed.

"He showed you?" Amber repeated and then looked back over at the stuffed animal to see the small lens hidden in his neckwear. "Waddle is a baby monitor?"

"He's an Amber monitor."

"And this is my nursery?" she asked in disbelief, quickly throwing off the vestiges of sleep.

"I think your Little is too old for a nursery although some pieces of furniture are the same. I think of this as your playroom."

"My Little is too old?" she repeated, realizing that she'd done that a lot today. Rio always seemed a few steps in front of her.

"Ready to talk?"

She nodded.

"Come sit on my lap," he invited and scooped her out of bed to carry her to the oversized rocker.

"Rio..." she began and then couldn't figure out what else to say.

"How about if I go first?"

When she nodded, he continued, "I've always been wired differently from others. Even from a young age, I needed to be in control, not to simply dominate, but to care for special people. When I found that book with everyone's notes in the margins, it confirmed what I already suspected—the popular head cheerleader who others relied on was actually a Little in disguise."

He brushed the hair back from her face and pressed a soft kiss to her lips. "I'm glad you had your friends for support when you discovered what you really needed to be happiest. Did reading that book scare you or arouse you?"

"Both. I always knew there were outgoing people and quiet people. I figured that's how everyone was in their relationships, too. I didn't know that the most in-control person could need to submit intimately."

"But you do. Not only for pleasure, but to restore your energy and love of life," Rio suggested.

"I've never found that, but I fantasize of finding someone who cares that much about me."

Amber couldn't believe she admitted that aloud. Somehow, here in his arms, she felt safe to express her most intimate dreams and needs.

"I think I can help you with that, Little girl." Rio rubbed her back reassuringly.

"So, what do we do?"

"First, we have lunch. Then we spend time together to get reacquainted with each other."

"We kind of put whipped cream and a cherry on top of the get-to-know-you part of our relationship today," she reminded him with sass.

"I will make love to you often, Ella. I need to be close to you," he said smoothly before continuing, "We need to set up some guidelines for our relationship and get you moved in here."

"You want me to live here?" she asked, running her fingers through the hair that flopped artfully over his brow.

"I need you to live here, Little girl, until they finish our house. I can't take care of you if you're not with me."

"You're not one of those possessive jerks that won't let their girl hang out with her friends, are you?"

"Jerk is not the right word for me. Depending on the type of hang out, I could be okay with you having some private time."

She looked at him skeptically. "Give me an example of an activity you would veto and one you'd approve."

"Going to the bar with friends and driving home after drinking—no. Being dropped off for a gathering of friends at someone's house and calling when you're ready to come home—yes."

That made sense. It actually sounded good. Amber avoided drinking because she felt wonky after one drink when it came to driving. If someone else was transporting her, she could relax and have a glass of wine or a margarita.

She dropped that argument because she had nothing to disagree with him about. Running over his list of things they should do, Amber seized on one word.

"What do you mean, guidelines?"

"Are you ready to get up?" he asked.

At her nod, Rio helped her stand before taking her hand. "Let's go get some lunch."

Once in the kitchen, Amber offered, "How can I help?"

"Sit down and talk to me."

"No, really. Put me to work. I'm glad to help."

"Little girls don't work at home. That's their Daddy's job. Allow me to take care of you, Ella," Rio requested.

What could she say to that? Nodding, Amber slid into a chair at the table. She answered Rio's questions about places she'd worked in over the years as she watched him deftly slice and dice some vegetables and cooked chicken before stir-frying them quickly with rice and some seasonings.

"That smells heavenly," she complimented.

"Good. I hope you'll enjoy the flavor as well. I do this a lot for myself. It's fast, easy, and can be nutritious."

"And it makes leftovers for the next day," she observed.

"Perfect for a Little girl's lunchbox for work."

"I usually just throw a handful of crackers and some cheese together in a plastic bag and call it good," she confessed. Amber couldn't imagine taking the time to make herself lunch each day.

"I'll make sure your lunch is ready for you to take," Rio promised as he spooned a healthy portion of the concoction into a large bowl and carried it over to place on the table between their chairs.

"You're not eating?" she asked in confusion.

"We'll start with this and get more if we're still hungry."

Rio dipped the fork in the fried rice and lifted it to her mouth. He waited for her to react with a hum of delight before smiling and taking a bite himself.

"You're an excellent cook," she complimented after swallowing before letting him feed her again.

An idea burst into her mind to add fun to the meal. "You don't have chopsticks, do you?"

"I do."

Rio returned to the kitchen and dug through a drawer to find a pair of bamboo sticks. "You feed us while I write," he instructed as he pulled a pad of paper close.

Feeling awkward, Amber fitted the utensils in her hand and scooped up a portion to offer to him. Rio opened his mouth and chuckled as a few grains of rice tumbled to the table.

"You're good at that. I would have dropped the whole darn thing on the floor."

Her embarrassment faded away. Rio was the same as he'd always been—fun and accepting of new things. With more confidence,

Amber tried the chopsticks again to feed herself before holding out a bite to him next. This time, she didn't drop a grain of rice.

Amber's gaze dropped to the paper as he wrote Guidelines at the top of the page.

"Guidelines?" she read aloud before taking another bite.

"It's a nicer word for rules," he explained. "I've thought of this a lot as I've waited to have you in my life. Here's what I would suggest."

Rio listed three items:

Guidelines

- Listen to each other.
- Pay attention to what matters.
- Daddy's in charge. His decisions trump everything else.

"That last one is a bit over the top, don't you think?" Amber asked with a laugh. *Surely, he's joking.*

"No."

"But you don't get to tell me what to do—always," Amber protested. "This is just during our play times, right?"

"Yes and no. A Little girl is always Little. You were Little at eighteen. You were Little for the last twenty years. And you'll be Little with me for the rest of your life. Being a Daddy or a Little isn't a game or a 'when I feel like it' kink. This is how we're wired."

"So, you just get to tell me what to do and I call you Daddy?" Amber railed, suddenly overwhelmed by the idea of losing her independence totally.

"Look at number one, please, and lower your voice. We don't yell at each other in this house."

"Maybe I should just leave then," Amber yelled louder and threw her chopsticks on the floor.

"I've waited for you to test your limits. You've found them," Rio announced. He set the pen down on the pad and pushed back his chair.

Plucking her from her seat, Rio stripped her jeans and panties quickly down her thighs before Amber could even react. She flailed her hands around, trying to stop him and reverse his actions, but Rio simply captured her wrists and held them behind her back as he continued.

"Stop, Rio! This isn't okay," she protested.

Immediately, he held her still. "Think carefully, Ella. Do you have the strength to live the fantasy that has consumed you for twenty years? Can you be brave enough to be Little?"

Silence stretched between them as she fidgeted in front of him. Amber was excruciatingly aware that she was partially undressed in the middle of his kitchen. "Are you going to spank me?" she finally whispered.

"Do you deserve it?"

Amber looked at the list of three guidelines. She'd failed miserably at the first two and panicked at the last one. Her dreams of having a Daddy always involved a stern protector. Shying away from reading the list again, Amber looked around the room. The hot, delicious meal he had created for her sat abandoned and cooling in the middle of the table. Her thrown chopsticks lay on the floor along with a few grains of rice needlessly wasted.

"Do you need to be spanked, Ella? To know what it feels like to be cared for by a man who accepts all of you and wants to help you deal with your feelings instead of panicking and running away?"

"I don't want to be spanked," she wailed, staring at the floor.

"Spankings wipe away all the bad feelings and worries."

"Promise?"

"Yes."

Amber stared at him as she processed through all that had happened so quickly. Her life felt like it had tumbled out of control. *Can I trust him?*

Rio had never lied to her. Even when she was a child, he'd told her the truth and explained it to her so she could understand. He hadn't spoiled her. Even then, he'd required that she behave.

He must have seen something in her face because he pulled her close to hug her tightly. When she relaxed against him, Rio said, "Let me help you, Little girl."

At her nod, he guided her across his lap. "Why are you getting a spanking, Amber?" he asked quietly as his hand smoothed over her bare bottom.

"I was awful," she confessed, on the verge of tears.

"What did you do, Ella?"

"I panicked at the idea that you'd always be in charge. I yelled and threw my chopsticks."

Without hesitating, his hand rose and dropped sharply on her bottom. Instant heat flashed through her skin, making Amber rear up from her drooped position over his hard thighs.

"Back in place, Little girl," he said quietly.

"That hurt."

"It will hurt more before it's time for your punishment to stop."

His complete matter-of-factness about spanking her made Amber relax back into position.

"Good girl."

Immediately, his hand landed on her exposed curves. Amber covered her face as tears gathered in her eyes. She bit her lip trying to convince herself that this wasn't working, but a sob broke through.

"Daddy's proud of you, Ella."

"Isn't that enough?" she pleaded. Her skin felt like it was on fire. She didn't want to look over her shoulder to see how red her skin was.

"Daddy's in charge. We'll both know when it's time for your spanking to end."

Rio's wide hand scattered swats over her bottom and that sensitive area at the top of her legs. Only able to concentrate on the sting, Amber dropped her hands from her face and let the tears fall to the carpet. The world seemed to shrink around them. Nothing else mattered.

"I'm sorry, Daddy," she whispered.

His hand paused and then rubbed her aching flesh. "Who's in charge, Little girl?"

"Daddy."

"Why?"

"Because that's the way it's supposed to be."

Rio scooped her up in his arms and cradled her body to his. Rocking her gently, he kissed her forehead before tucking her head on his shoulder.

"What are you worried about?" he probed.

"My poor bottom?" She attempted a joke and then searched her thoughts. Amber always had some concern in the back of her head, whether it had to do with work, her parents, or the upcoming move. Now her thoughts focused only on one thing—their relationship.

Her sore bottom was so worth it to put everything in perspective. She tangled her fingers in Rio's T-shirt and tugged slightly. "I won't need a spanking often. I'm not a brat," she assured him.

"I agree. You are a very sweet Little girl who needs to learn she now has a safe place to be herself and let someone else take care of all the things that suck the joy out of life."

"My Daddy?"

"Exactly. Your Daddy will handle everything if you'll allow him to."

Amber lifted her head and looked at that pad of paper on the table. This time, as she read it, her mind didn't panic. They sounded very positive. "I like those guidelines."

That earned her a kiss on the head and a hug. Wrapping an arm around her to hold her on his lap, Rio scooted back to the table. "Can I have another bite, Amberella?"

She looked at the dirty chopsticks on the floor and then over at the original utensil he'd scooted to the side. It wouldn't be as fun as the chopsticks had been. "Can I use the fork?"

"Of course," Rio answered, handing it to her.

As she scooped up a bite for him, Rio wrote the next few lines. When he turned his face toward her, she fed him a forkful of the mixture.

"Thank you. Now, you."

She ate a bite. It wasn't piping hot like before, but it was almost as good. Amber chewed happily before looking at what he had finished.

Punishments

- Spanking
- Corner time
- Daddy's choice

"Daddy's choice?" she questioned.

"Exactly."

Amber considered pushing him for more information but decided maybe she didn't want to know. "I'll just be good, and I'll never find out," she suggested.

"Good plan," he encouraged and took the fork from her hand to scoop up a portion of the delicious concoction. Rio lifted it to her lips and at the last moment, turned the fork to zoom it into his mouth, leaving Amber with her mouth open. The twinkle of merriment in his eyes made her giggle.

"Daddy!"

CHAPTER 13

After gathering all her possessions from her parents' house and moving everything to Rio's place, Amber dressed for the fancy reunion dinner in the late afternoon. Her shapewear made the cocktail dress look amazing, but it compressed her punished bottom, reminding her to be very good.

She was putting the final touches on her makeup when her phone rang. Amber smiled at the name on her phone as she answered it, putting it on speaker so she could continue getting ready.

"Harper! Are you heading over to the reunion?" she asked.

"We're walking out the door right now." Harper's sweet voice sounded nervous.

"Be ready for some questions," Amber warned.

"Just give me a hug instead," Harper whispered.

"Fifteen minutes, Amber. Meet you there," Colt called from close by.

"I'm putting my shoes on. Rio's driving me."

"Tell me he's wearing a suit," Harper demanded.

"He's wearing a suit."

"Damn. See you soon." Harper ended the call.

"Does Harper have a thing about suits?" Rio's deep voice said from the doorway into the magical room where he stowed her suitcase.

Amber whirled around with her stilettos in hand to see him. Her gaze ran over the perfectly tailored suit that revealed his athletic form and concealed his tattoos. Rio looked like a very wealthy, very successful business executive. "Goodness. You are a banker," she said, walking toward him.

"My father almost approves of my appearance these days when I have to work at the bank," Rio shared, straightening his cuffs so only a hint of the gorgeous tattoos that decorated his forearms showed. He raised his pant leg a few inches to display his red socks.

"Your father is a fool." Amber offered him her mouth for a kiss.

When he lifted his head, she smiled. "That was totally worth messing up my lipstick for."

"You can fix it in the car. Let's go. Your friends are waiting. Let me help."

Rio knelt on one knee at her feet and ran an admiring hand from the modest hem of her fitted cocktail dress to one foot. Plucking the fancy shoes from her hand, he slid each one over her toes and into place before standing to admire the picture she presented.

"I am a very lucky Daddy," he admitted, stepping forward to wrap a hand around her waist and guide her to the door. "You might make it to our bed before that dress is on the floor."

What could she say to that? Rio was a very sensual man. She had no doubt he wouldn't hesitate to make love to her wherever they happened to be.

"Are you really building a house on that spot?" Amber asked.

"The builder is meeting me out there on Monday to get started," Rio told her as he buckled her safely into his sports car parked in the garage next to her snazzy ride that now occupied one space.

When they arrived at the venue hosting the reunion gathering, Amber tried to wait patiently for Rio to park and come around the car to unlock the door. When he opened it, she burst from the car and started walking immediately toward the side door where the group of friends had promised to meet. She could see everyone had already arrived.

"Ella."

Amber stopped in her tracks, recognizing that as the only warning she would receive. She looked over her shoulder to see Rio walking slowly toward her. When he reached her, he held out his hand for hers and then continued his same deliberate pace with Amber, protecting her from traffic by his body.

"Damn," Colt's voice called across the last few yards as they approached. "I don't know who's prettier—Amber or Rio."

"Amber, of course," Rio corrected him before shaking hands with Colt and Beau as the ladies hugged everyone.

"Harper, that dress is gorgeous. It didn't come from Avondale," Amber suggested, scanning her friend's beautiful appearance.

"I might have treated myself to a trip out of town," Harper confessed.

"It's so flattering," Maisie added. "You look curvalicious. Someone can't keep his eyes off you." She nodded Colt's way.

When all three ladies looked, they saw his gaze was locked on Harper. Amber couldn't wait to get a chance to talk to Harper alone. She made plans to waylay her after the reunion was finished.

"Shall we go in? I have a feeling this group is eagerly anticipated," Rio suggested.

Creating nametags for themselves at the welcome table, Rio easily smoothed over the fact that Amber had only registered for one dinner, paying for another meal. His handsome appearance and perfect manners charmed the class member dealing with the hotel staff, who assured him there would be no problem with a last-minute addition.

Quickly, they claimed a table before they were mobbed by classmates who wished to talk to the famous country star, Colt, the rising politician, Beau, and the handsome man accompanying Amber. The three women looked at the swarm surrounding the men and shrugged.

"Glass of wine, ladies?" Maisie suggested.

Rio caught Amber's eye and excused himself from those around him. "What are you drinking, ladies?"

"I guess wine," Harper answered. "I'm not really good with choosing the right kind."

"Allow me," Rio said with a wink and asked, "Red or white, tart or sweet?"

"Red, sweet," Amber answered.

"White, sweet," Maisie selected.

"Surprise me?" Harper suggested.

"Got it. I'll be right back."

By the time Rio returned from the bar with a tray of drinks he'd confiscated from somewhere, Beau and Colt had extricated themselves from those wishing to ask a million questions. He passed out the wine to each woman, handed a beer to Colt, a glass of scotch to Beau, and a sparkling glass of something for himself.

"Cheers, everyone," Rio suggested, raising his glass. The others echoed his salute and tasted their beverages.

"The best wine ever," Amber announced, taking another sip.

"Nope, it's in my glass," Maisie corrected her.

Harper just tapped on her glass and pointed with a smile to state her opinion.

"Thanks for showing us up, Rio," Colt joked, lightly slapping Rio on the arm.

"I'll share the names if you want to grab a few bottles," he offered.

"I'd like that. Thanks," Beau answered, taking another sip of the golden alcohol in his glass.

"So, we've talked about what we've been doing for the last twenty years. What are everyone's plans for the next five or more?" Amber asked.

"Now that Harper and I are together, we have big decisions to make," Colt shared, hugging Harper to his body.

"*Together*, together?" Maisie asked skeptically.

"Together," Colt assured her.

"Congratulations," Amber rushed to say, seeing Harper looking increasingly more self-conscious.

"Thank you," Harper whispered.

"I'll be in a think tank with a bunch of brainiacs who consume too many energy drinks," Maisie informed them drily.

"Maisie, how far are you from the Capitol building?"

"No one lives in DC. I'm in Alexandria, Virginia. It's a quick drive if you commute at four in the morning," she joked.

"I don't suppose you have a room to rent if I win the election?" Beau asked in a very normal tone that caught everyone's attention.

"A room to rent?" Maisie echoed, staring at Beau as if he'd grown a second head.

"I'm moving in with Rio," Amber announced, taking the heat off Beau.

"Really?" Harper squeaked. "I can't tell you how happy I am that you're working at the hospital."

"I'll maintain a home here and spend time here when we are on breaks," Beau pointed out. "The only person who won't be officially living in town will be Maisie. I think she could do her think tank thing here."

"Lots of people are doing things remotely," Colt pointed out.

"Slow down, everyone. I have no intention of moving back to this judgy town. No matter if I create a cure for the common cold or grow a fully functional human heart, I'll always be the trailer trash from the wrong side of the tracks," she said, smoothing the elegantly fitted cocktail dress into place.

"Looks like she's going to be a challenge," Colt suggested.

"Definitely," Beau confirmed.

Maisie glared at her two grinning friends in an epic stare down. It shouldn't have been a challenge with Maisie having to divide her time between the two men, but she held her own. No one could ever accuse Maisie of not being spunky.

"Perhaps you should come back to visit more often," Beau suggested softly.

"I don't remember this hunk being part of our class. Were you, like, the shop teacher?" a familiar catty voice asked.

Everyone turned to consider the unpleasant woman who had

joined them. Miranda was determined to maintain the status quo from high school. Unfortunately for her, everyone else had moved on.

"I'm assuming you're referring to me?" Rio asked. "I never attended Avondale High School."

"I didn't think so. I would have remembered you," Miranda assured him, moving closer.

Bristling, Amber opened her mouth to say something, but Rio simply pulled her a bit closer to his side and patted her hip. His focus on her didn't please Miranda. Thank goodness, their class president chose that moment to welcome everyone and ask people to take their seats.

"Do not allow others' unhappiness to affect your life," Rio whispered into her ear as he assisted Amber into her chair at the table. A light kiss against her temple reinstated her good mood.

After an unremarkable banquet meal, the band started to play, and Rio stood to offer his hand to Amber. She hesitated, looking at the empty dance floor, not wanting to be the center of attention. When Beau and Colt stood as well, Amber nodded at the other women, offering encouragement, and stood.

As she stepped onto the parquet floor, Rio swept her elegantly into his arms. Skillfully leading her into a simple pattern of steps that she grew more confident in following, Rio made her feel like a fairy princess.

"Is there anything you don't do well?" she asked.

"My Italian is atrocious," he admitted.

"But your French is skilled, hmm?" Amber teased.

"Fairly good. I went to Paris when I left Avondale. My mother's family still lives there. I bartended at night and took accounting classes during the day," he shared.

"Really?" she asked, filing this away to ask for more details. Rio was such a complex person. Would she ever know everything about him?

A thought bounced into her mind. "You work for the De Leon banks now. Avondale is too small for a branch here, I'd guess."

"Yes. Like Maisie, I do much of my work online, but I will have several onsite visits to make throughout the year. Depending on your work schedule, you'll have to join me," he suggested.

"Fun places?" she asked.

"Is Paris fun?" he asked, then balanced her skillfully when she stumbled over her steps.

"Yes. Paris would be fun."

"Then you'll go with me on my next trip. I would be delighted to show you such a beautiful city."

"I don't even know what to say," Amber murmured, trying to look like she wasn't completely flabbergasted. "I have so much to learn about you."

"And I you. The next twenty years should be interesting, hmm?" he suggested, drawing her into a beautiful turn to finish the music.

CHAPTER 14

When they walked into Rio's beautiful house after dinner and dancing, Amber collapsed to the couch to take off her shoes as Rio slung his jacket over the back of a nearby chair. Kneeling at her feet, Rio shooed her hands away and lifted her leg to slide the stiletto from her foot. He rubbed her instep, easing the tension away from standing on the high heels before repeating his attentions to the other foot as Amber tried to control her moans of delight.

"I'll give you a few hours to stop that," Amber joked as he settled on the couch next to her with her feet in his lap, obviously meaning to continue his attention to her.

"Maybe I need to add another guideline to our list. Should heels be outlawed? Little girls don't need to wear them."

"No, Rio. I need some big girl time, too. I promise I won't prance around in them every day. Just like I won't wear this fancy dress or this shapewear for a long time," she said, reaching under the hem to snap the restrictive garment underneath.

Without saying a word, Rio stood and tugged her to stand in front of him. Deftly, he stripped off her dress and undergarments. "This is unacceptable," he murmured, tracing a red mark on her skin.

"You're going to go crazy when you see what happens to me working at the hospital," she told him, trying to distract herself from being self-conscious as she stood in front of him naked.

"You will be careful," he warned.

"I promise."

Without another word, Rio scooped her into his arms and carried her through the house to the large master bathroom. After setting her feet gently on the soft rug in front of one basin at the vanity, Rio turned on the faucet to let water gush into the bathtub.

Amber reached for her toothbrush in the holder that held his as well. It seemed very intimate to have something so ordinary together. Only one thing remained in her suitcase. Amber wondered if she'd be brave enough to get him when it was time for bed.

She brushed her teeth as she watched Rio unbutton his dress shirt and remove his cufflinks before shrugging out of the garment and tossing it into the basket for dry-cleaning. Scanning his powerful body, Amber tried to tamp down her arousal. When he removed his slacks and boxer briefs, she forgot to move the toothbrush in her mouth. Catching herself, Amber quickly finished and rinsed her mouth.

Approaching the bath to see if the water was deep enough to sit down in and to stop herself from staring at him, Amber discovered she could see his reflection perfectly in a mirror positioned over the tub. *Damn, he's pretty.*

"Thank you, Ella."

Embarrassed that she had actually said that aloud, Amber stepped one foot quickly into the tub and then hopped out, dancing in discomfort with one red foot. Rio knelt at her feet within a fraction of a second to make sure she was okay.

"It's fine. I should have noticed the steam rising from the water," she told him.

"You need to learn to wait for Daddy's permission, Little girl. Your bath was not ready," he scolded her.

"Rio, I'm not used to asking for permission to get in the bathtub," Amber said mockingly.

"Daddy," he corrected her with a stern look before reaching up to adjust the water temperature.

"I suppose I get spanked," she said flippantly.

"No bubbles," he announced.

Inside, she regretted losing them even though the idea hadn't popped into her mind. How did he know that would be a negative consequence? "Fine," she answered as if that were nothing.

Rio didn't answer but checked the bathwater. "It's safe now. Do you want me to get in first to make sure?"

"You're taking a bath with me?"

"I am."

She looked at the immense tub and tried to figure out where she needed to sit if they were both going to be inside at the same time. "You go first."

Rio stepped into the tub and sat down against the sloping back of the tub. He held his hand out to help her get in safely.

Tentatively, Amber dipped her toe into the water. This time it felt warm but okay to her. Rio reached up to steady her with a hand on each side of her hips. Realizing what a view he had of her body, she sank quickly into the water, regretting the loss of the bubbles even more.

"I was embarrassed," she blurted.

"For saying I was pretty?" he teased.

"That was supposed to stay in my head."

"Even Daddies need compliments sometimes. That is now officially my favorite one," he announced. "I may need a T-shirt with that on it."

Amber couldn't help but laugh at the mental image in her mind. When Rio joined her merriment, she relaxed. How did he always know how to make her feel better?

Rio reached for a large misshapen sponge and dipped it into the water. Adding a squeeze of liquid soap from a beautiful container on the ledge bordering the wall, he rubbed it against his chest to get it foamy before taking her hand and washing her arm.

"Lean back and relax, sweetheart. You've had quite a day."

With a sigh of delight, Amber followed his directions. She loved the way her Daddy took care of her.

Her Daddy. Amber repeated that in her mind. How could that feel so right in such a short period of time? Peeking through her lashes at Rio, she debated whether she should fight these feelings.

"It isn't often in life that we get second chances," Rio said softly as he washed her breasts and torso. She fought the allure of the sponge moving over her nipples and sensitive flesh to listen to his words and meaning.

"When I left and returned to take over my role in the family business, I knew I couldn't be assured that this day would come."

"You could have stayed," she suggested.

"Look back at everything you have done since high school graduation. Would you dismiss everything? If I had stayed, would you have made the same choices?"

Silent, she sat thinking as he washed her other arm. She would have never left him to go to North Carolina for school. Amber had already debated that from the moment she opened the acceptance letter.

Flashes from all the challenges she'd overcome and the fun she'd had traveling and meeting new people circled through her mind. Amber had enjoyed her adventures completely as she tried to ignore that something was missing from her life.

Amber knew she was in a totally different phase of her life. The pain of packing and moving now overwhelmed her love of trying out a new city and hospital. Being a traveling nurse had been exciting and challenging at first. Owning the bar and grill, her parents had never taken time off to travel or go on vacation. On her own after graduation, Amber had gotten to experience a variety of climates and communities. The allure of that was over. Now, she wanted to settle down in one place—with one person. Him.

"No," she answered simply. "I wouldn't be the same person if I hadn't done all the things I wanted to."

"Exactly. You needed a chance to spread your wings."

Rio straightened her leg over his thigh to stroke the lather over her skin. "There is thirteen years between our ages, Ella. Does that bother you?"

"No. It never has. You feel right."

"That pleases me."

"More than being pretty?" she asked to lighten their conversation.

"Even more than pretty," he agreed with a smile. "Come sit in front of me."

With his assistance, Amber shifted in the tub, taking a place between his outstretched thighs. She gathered her hair into a clump on the top of her head as he washed her back and earned a kiss on the side of her neck.

With the suds rinsed from her skin, Rio gently pulled her shoulders back to rest against his strength. Supporting her with an arm around her waist as she lay at a slight angle, he stroked the sponge down the center of her body.

"Spread your thighs, Little girl," he requested and stroked over her pussy when she quickly complied.

The feel of the soft material gliding over her intimately made her gasp quietly. Amber widened her legs, silently requesting a more intimate touch. To her delight, he was very thorough. She squirmed against him as he explored her pink folds before moving lower to clean between her buttocks. Squeezing that small ring of muscles as the sponge moved slowly over it, Amber held her breath.

"I plan to explore every inch of your body, Little girl."

Letting the sponge drift away, Rio teased her with his fingertips. She tried to sit up to guard her bottom from his touch, but Rio held her in position.

"There is nothing off limits to our passion," he growled into her ear. His fingertip circled the small entrance and pressed firmly against it as Amber froze in place.

Her arousal skyrocketed at this forbidden touch. His fingertip dipped inside. Amber closed her eyes as the sensations from this nerve-rich area overwhelmed her.

"I think I'll keep a small plug here by the tub. It can go in that decorative box right there," he suggested as he moved his fingertip in and out. "When I give you a bath, I can slide it into your bottom to tease you as you play in the tub. Maybe you'll want some crayons to draw pretty pictures on the side of the tub or your skin?"

"Daddy," she breathed.

"Do you need something, Ella?"

"Touch me," she whispered.

His finger slid a bit further inside her, making her gasp. "No. Not there," she pleaded as he continued his probing strokes.

"I think your protests might be unwarranted. You're enjoying my touch here, aren't you?"

"No," she wailed, trying to pull her legs together.

"Legs apart," he ordered.

Automatically, Amber followed his stern warning and his finger moved further inside. Each time it pushed through her tight opening, she felt a rush of arousal.

"What would I find if I touched your pussy, Ella? Is it slick with your juices? Would it reveal how aroused you are?" he asked.

"Yes," she whispered.

"Who's in charge, Little girl?"

"Daddy!"

"Why?"

"Because you know what I need," she admitted in a rush of words.

"Good girl," he praised her.

When his finger slid fully from her body, Amber's eyelids flashed back open. He wasn't going to leave her on the edge, was he? She clasped her legs back together as he sat her back up in the tub. Turning sideways, she watched him quickly clean his hands and rinse the water from the tub.

The liquid streamed off his fully aroused body as he stood. Rio's body revealed the effect of his dominance over her. Amber couldn't help but feel a bit of power. She'd caused that. It dawned on her that her submission was as stimulating to him as was his power over her.

When he stepped from the tub to wrap a towel around his waist, Amber waited quietly. Her confidence that he would care for her grew with every moment they spent together.

"Come here, Little girl," he directed, holding out an oversized cloth.

She rose from the tub and allowed him to dry her body. The feel of the terry fabric between her legs proved to be a challenge to resist. A needy moan escaped from her lips.

"You need my attention, don't you, Ella? Little girls always sleep better when their bodies are happy." He guided her into the master bedroom with an arm around her waist. Tugging back the covers on one side of the big bed, he invited, "Lie back against the pillows."

Climbing eagerly into bed, Amber settled into place and held out her arms. To her astonishment, he shook his head.

"I'm not ready to come to bed yet, Amberella. But you have my full attention. Spread your legs."

He's not coming to bed? She stared at him as her brain processed his words.

Rio repeated, "Spread your legs."

Amber slowly moved her thighs apart as she watched him stand close. His gaze focused completely on her nude body.

"Touch yourself, Ella. Make yourself come."

"You're... You're going to watch?" she stammered.

"You have my full attention, Little girl."

His words repeated in her mind. *"You need my attention, don't you, Ella? Little girls always sleep better when their bodies are happy."*

Her face heated and Amber knew she had turned a variety of shades of red and pink. She couldn't prevent the gush of arousal that coated her inner thighs with slick juices. He could see everything. Slowly, she glided one hand over her stomach and down to the silky hair guarding her pussy. Pulling slightly on the strands, Amber loved the slight taste of pain that distracted her.

Lowering her fingers, she stroked over her delicate folds, seeking those sensitive places that always tingled as she touched them. Her fingers were instantly wet. Daringly, she pressed one finger inside.

Walking forward, Rio opened the nightstand drawer and removed a small bottle before resuming his position at the bottom of the bed. Tossing the container on the bed, Rio stroked his hand over the erection tenting the towel around him. Her fingers fluttered against herself at the carnal move.

Unable to look away, she watched him lean against the side of the bed and unfasten the towel around his hips. His hand closed around the root of his cock and pulled hard down to the tip as Amber circled a fingertip around her clit, making her quiver inside. She increased her caresses as he grabbed the lubricant and squeezed some into his palm.

Amber's breath came faster as her inhibitions vanished. She could only concentrate on the pleasure she gave herself and the display he created for her. The feel of his gaze on her pussy felt almost physical. In her imagination, her touch became his. She plunged two fingers deep and circled her clit simultaneously. With a cry, she climaxed, falling apart before him.

With a shout into the room, Rio poured himself into the towel, He braced himself against the mattress, giving himself a moment to recover as her fingers slowed against her body.

"Very good, Little girl," he praised her as he moved to pull the covers up to her chin and press a kiss to her forehead.

Suddenly exhausted, Amber turned to her side and closed her eyes. She could hear him move around the room, placing the vial in the nightstand and placing the towel in the hamper. Amber wrapped her arms around herself. She wanted to go to sleep but something was missing.

When he started to get into bed to join her, she whispered, "Daddy, I need my stuffie. Can I go get it?"

"I'll go get it for you, sweetheart. Is it in your bag in the playroom?"

She nodded against the pillows. He left the room and returned holding a faded, obviously well-loved lime wedge. Amber slid her hand out of the covers to reach for Limey. "Thank you," she whispered. "I named him Limey."

"That's a perfect name. I'm glad you kept him, Little girl," Rio answered softly as he tucked the covers back around her.

In a few seconds, he had the dim lights turned off . Closing her eyes, she crashed into sleep.

She roused slightly when he slid into bed a couple hours later. His arm wrapped around Amber and Limey to pull them against his warmth. As she nestled close to him, she mumbled, "Night, night, Daddy."

"Night, Little girl."

Amber felt his lips press against her temple and she fell back asleep with him wrapped around her—warm, protected, and feeling loved.

CHAPTER 15

Waking up the next morning in Rio's arms felt so right. Amber cuddled against his chest and absorbed the happiness that seemed to come with being near the dynamic man. When his hand smoothed over her back, she pressed a kiss against his chest before looking up at him.

"Good morning, Little girl. Did you have fun last night at the reunion?" he asked with a smile.

"I had an amazing time. Thank you for going with me."

"Of course. I have always enjoyed your friends. They're definitely interesting now that they've grown up."

"Everyone at school never could understand why we were friends. We just clicked. Then when we found that book, I figured it was because we were all Littles and Daddies," Amber suggested.

"That's a definite possibility. I think you're all very loyal personalities as well and you truly care about each other."

"That's true. I'd love if everyone ended back here together. I didn't realize how much I missed them. I mean, we talk on video from time to time—but less as time passes."

"You came home. I have a suspicion Colt bought the property adjacent to mine. I tried to buy the parcel of land closer to town, but it had already been claimed."

"That would be such a coincidence," she answered skeptically.

"Definitely. He hasn't said anything about it. I'd suggest we let him share the news without mentioning my suspicion to Harper."

"Okay," she said with a shrug. A few seconds passed while they were each lost in their own thoughts.

"What are we doing today?" Amber asked, propping an arm across Rio's broad chest.

"I'd like you to look at my house plans and see if there is anything you'd like to include or take out."

"I don't know how valid my opinion is. My architectural skills are limited. I always wanted a big outdoor space with a pizza oven," she confessed.

"We can make that happen. I think we'll need an entertainment space for your friends. They'll all need a refuge to escape to."

"And pizza!" she teased and then squealed as he reversed their positions to lie above her.

"Now I know the way to your heart. Dough, cheese, and sauce." Rio leaned down to kiss her deeply.

"And hot pepper sprinkles," she reminded him when he lifted his head. Unable to resist, she brushed her fingers through his sleep-tousled hair.

"Spice is important to life," he answered.

"And limes?" she asked, catching a glimpse of Limey, who'd somehow ended up tucked between Rio's pillow and the headboard.

"You boinked me over the head with Limey about two in the morning," he informed her.

"Limey gets rambunctious sometimes. He didn't hurt you, did he?"

"No, Ella. Limey and I are old friends."

"I've loved him since you left him for me."

"I'm glad. I wanted you to have something to hold on to as you left to go explore the world."

"Did you mean what you said? That we could travel to Paris some day?"

"When do you report for work?"

"I gave myself two weeks to get settled and find some place to live before I start."

"That item is already checked off your list," he announced with a firm glance. "Let's go tomorrow. We could spend a few days and return with time for you to unpack when your things arrive and be ready for work."

"What am I going to do with all my furniture?" Amber blurted as she remembered her storage cube would come next week with all her belongings.

"We'll put it in storage until you decide what you want to keep. This place came furnished."

"You don't have any furniture?" she asked as the beautiful room she'd napped in flashed into her mind.

"A few things. The original items that occupied space in your playroom are in the basement. Everything there now belongs to us," he assured her.

"I'm glad. I seriously love that room. Did you mean what you said? We could go to Paris?"

"Do you have a passport with you?"

"In a file in my car. There were a few documents I thought I needed to keep with me."

"Then I will arrange for tickets when we get up."

"Really? We have to get ready if we're going tomorrow. I don't think I have the right clothes," she worried. Pushing his shoulders away, she sat up to look at him.

"We can buy anything we need, Little girl. Unless you plan to go to L'Opera, I think you'll be fine in jeans. A couple of nice dresses for dinner would be appropriate."

Amber flung herself over Rio's body to scatter kisses on his face. "I'm so excited."

"I can tell, Ella. Shall we get up and make some plans?"

"Yes!"

Flinging the covers off, Amber instantly shivered as cool air enveloped her nude body. She dragged the sheet back over herself as Rio chuckled. "I usually wear pajamas."

"I'll keep that in mind when I tuck you in bed at night," he promised, sitting up to pull her to his warmth. "Although I don't mind having your skin next to mine all night."

"I liked it, too," she admitted before grinning at him. "Paris!"

"Let's get up and order tickets before you explode, Amberella. I can't wait to show you Paris."

* * *

THREE DAYS LATER, Amber sat next to the most handsome man in the world at a café on the Champs-Elysées.

"*Et voila, Madame,*" the indulgent French waiter pronounced as he poured a large amount of rich cream into her coffee cup to create the *grande crème* that she had become quite fond of already. Amber had been concerned that she wouldn't be able to doll up her coffee with her customary four creamers and sugar, but leave it to the French to have the perfect concoction already, and for her Daddy to know what to order.

"*Merci, infiniment,*" Amber thanked him with her very limited French that Rio had taught her. She didn't miss the glance he exchanged with her Daddy as he turned to leave.

"Don't tell me… He's a Daddy?" she asked with a raised eyebrow.

"Quite possibly, Little girl. Or perhaps just a Frenchmen who appreciates beautiful women. This is the city of love after all."

"Thank you for bringing me here. Paris is all I dreamed it would be."

"I'm glad, Ella. I have enjoyed seeing it through your eyes."

"What are we doing today, Rio?" Amber asked before changing the name to "Daddy?" when he looked at her sternly.

"I thought we'd visit the bar I worked at when I was here years ago after we head up there." He pointed to a white building perched on a high hill. "Montmartre provides a gorgeous workspace for many artists."

"Will we get to visit the Louvre?" she asked, leaning forward eagerly. "I want to see the *Mona Lisa*."

"Of course. I think we'll see that tomorrow. Then, I'll take you to a smaller museum I prefer. There are a couple of rooms there I know you'll enjoy."

"Really? More than the *Mona Lisa*?" she asked.

"I think so," he said with a small smile that made her expect he would be right. Even after years apart, Rio knew her at her core.

"I've been thinking about those plans you showed me on the way over," she said hesitantly.

"Yes. Did you think of something we need to change?"

"Is there any way my playroom could be off the master bedroom?"

"You'd feel more comfortable having it be more private? Just for you and me to know about?" he asked.

Amber nodded and waited.

"I think that is a very good idea. I will ask the architect to put in an extra-large dressing area attached to our bedroom. I'll send him a note today and ask him to revamp the floor plans to allow for that."

"Can it have a window seat for me? I always dreamed of having one to sit and read in."

"Of course," Rio agreed, pulling out his phone and making notes. He'd already jotted down their desire for an outdoor kitchen area with a pizza oven and seating for at least eight.

Her mind wandered as he sent a detailed message to the architect. When an idea popped into her mind, she asked, "Do you think anyone you remember will still be at the bar you worked at?"

"I won't know until I get there. Perhaps not, and we'll just have a glass of good French wine before choosing a restaurant for dinner. You don't mind going with me, do you?"

"No. I'd like to see where you worked."

"Perfect."

Riding the Metro was an experience. Thank goodness Rio knew how to plot their destination on the interwoven subway lines. Amber hid her grin when her Daddy discovered that during his absence, the stations had updated to completely automated ticket sales instead of attendants at the windows. It had taken him several attempts to figure out how to order tickets.

They walked up the cobblestone streets leading to Sacré-Coeur, the gleaming white church that sat on the top of the hill. Small shops and cafés lined the way along with artists at their easels crafting beautiful creations as people watched.

A man finishing a portrait of a small child caught Amber's attention. It was a remarkable likeness that captured not just the outward appearance of the toddler but a spark of life.

When she lingered watching, Rio suggested, "Shall we have him draw us?"

"Oh, that has to be expensive." She tried to brush his suggestion aside.

"You have not asked for a single souvenir to take home. I think my wallet can handle this."

Rio turned to talk to the artist who immediately seized on the opportunity to create something special for them. Rio sat in the chair carefully placed next to the easel and scooped Amber into his lap. As they sat, he regaled her with funny stories of the people he'd met in Paris.

Amber had almost forgotten about the artist who worked silently next to them until he announced, *"Fini!"*

Rio helped her off his lap and they rounded the canvas to look at the finished project. Her heart leapt in her chest to see the expression of happiness and laughter on their faces. The artist had captured them perfectly. Rio looked devastatingly handsome with his silvery black hair and dark eyes. And Amber looked lovelier than she'd ever thought of being. They looked right together.

Amber glanced up at Rio and tucked her hand into his. Delighted to have such a personal memento of their time together, she squeezed his hand and turned to thank the artist.

He responded with a fast slew of French that she couldn't hope to understand. Rio, however, answered with a smile as he handed over the euros plus a tip for the artist. When the portrait was securely rolled into a protective tube, Rio guided Amber back onto the path.

"I love this," she said, clutching the cardboard to her chest.

"You chose wisely, Little girl. It helps that he was captivated by you as he worked. He was very inspired to capture your likeness," Rio shared.

"How sweet. I liked him, too."

When they'd finished exploring the artistic area, Rio guided her back down the hill to conquer the subway system once again. "Let's stop for a drink and some lunch at Harry's."

"That sounds very American."

"Oh, it is. An American shipped a New York bar to Paris and put it back together here. It was a fun place to work."

Getting off at the L'Opera stop, Rio told her all he knew about the gorgeous gilt-embellished building as they passed it. When they reached the bustling bar, Rio took her hand and led her into the crowd.

She turned to look when a man called, "*Voici* Rio!" and tossed a white apron his way.

Amber let the French tumble over her without even attempting to understand as employees came from all sides to hug and exchange the traditional kisses to the cheeks. As Rio introduced her, she was surprised to be swept up in the celebration when everyone greeted her with equal enthusiasm.

She hovered by his side as he held her hand to ensure she wasn't lost in the crowd. A woman carrying a tray swept past to deliver food to a table before returning to stand near Amber.

"So, it was you he left to grow up?" she asked in English with a hint of a Parisian accent.

"Pardon me?"

"Rio told us he'd left the US so the one he loved would have every opportunity to live her best life. That was you, wasn't it?"

"Yes."

"And you are together now?" the server demanded.

"Yes."

"Good. I always told him he was an idiot."

"You haven't changed a bit, Eloise!" Rio said, stepping forward to hug the attractive woman to his chest.

"Sit there. I will bring you your favorites," Eloise ordered.

"And a glass of Bordelaise for Amber," he requested quietly.

"Of course. I'm glad to see you together, Rio."

Amber watched her Daddy hug the woman once again before following him to the table Eloise had indicated. She guessed that when Rio had been here before, they would have made a very eye-catching couple. Amber didn't get any romantic vibes from the two of them—just companionable ones.

"Did you two date?" she asked, unable to resist the urge to double-check her hunch.

"No. Eloise is as dominant as I am. Her Little boy works here at the bar. You'll pick up on their relationship soon if you watch," Rio assured her with a smile.

It took a while. Amber was halfway through her delicious wine when she saw it. Eloise patted the bottom of a huge man restocking the bar with a giant keg of something alcoholic. There looked to be the same age gap between them as her and Rio.

"He's the owner?" Amber asked, leaning forward to talk to Rio privately.

"He is now. When I was here before, he was the youngest son of the owner. He took one glance at Eloise and it was over. They've been together for years."

"I'm sorry we lost so many years we could have been together," she said, feeling sad.

"Our path was different. I don't plan to be separated from you again."

"Even to come work here? I bet it was fun."

"It occupied my time. I needed to be busy," he shared. "Enough of the past. Our time is growing short in Paris for this trip. Let's go change for dinner."

CHAPTER 16

For their last day in Paris, Rio had promised her something special. Amber couldn't imagine that this small museum could hold anything more special than the Louvre with its vast collection of world-famous masterpieces. She followed him into a room and stopped in disbelief.

"Daddy?" Amber whispered in awe before turning in a slow circle to take in the beauty surrounding her.

"This room and the next inspired your playroom. I sat in here for hours and planned for time I hoped to have with you."

She collapsed onto one of the padded benches as people walked through the room admiring the huge panels that lined the oval wall. "Who painted these?"

"Monet. These are four landscapes from his waterlily collection. He crafted them from the grounds of his Giverny estate."

"I want to go there," she breathed, taking in the incredible display of colors flowing together.

"Next time," he promised.

"My room has more green," she whispered.

"Your favorite color is green," he reminded her.

"How do you remember all those things about me?" she asked. "I don't have a clue what color you like."

"Pink."

She blinked at him. "Really?" Pink seemed way too girly for such a masculine man.

"Truly," he promised, plucking at the deep rose-colored T-shirt that hugged his chest.

Amber nodded. She'd decided she liked pink a lot more than she normally would when he'd pulled that garment on this morning. "It fits you."

They sat there quietly for several minutes. She appreciated that he didn't rush her at all, but instead allowed her to rotate on the bench to look at each of the four paintings surrounding her.

"There's another room?" she asked when she thought she'd memorized everything.

"Let's go see it. Then perhaps, you'd like to pick up a book in the gift shop."

"Yes, please."

A couple of hours after their entrance, she forced herself to leave. "I can't believe they had a coloring book as well." Amber almost skipped with excitement. The kind shopkeeper had even produced a set of colored pencils with a wide display of colors. That would make the long flight home so much more enjoyable.

"And a raspberry beret for you as well," Rio said, tweaking the slouchy hat perched on her head.

"Because you like pink, Daddy."

They walked along in silence for several minutes, each lost in their thoughts.

"Why now, Rio? Why did you come back to Avondale now?"

"You were there. It was time to see if you'd forgotten the guy behind the bar or if I was right that we had something special."

"And if I'd been married with kids in high school?"

"I would have remembered you fondly and dreamed of what might have been."

"You wouldn't have fought for me?" Amber stopped abruptly in the middle of the sidewalk.

Rio steered her to the side and stood protecting her from being bumped by other pedestrians. "I would not have ripped apart a family if you were happy with someone else."

Amber studied his face. No, Rio would have never done that. He'd only ever wanted her to be happy. "It killed you to leave, didn't it?"

"Yes."

"Then we need to make the most of our time together now."

Amber pushed her regret of not having Rio in her life for so long out of her heart and mind for the last time. She wouldn't waste time thinking about what coulda, woulda, shoulda been. It was time to enjoy having him in her life.

"Could we go back to our room for a nap?" she asked, peeking up at him.

"A nap or something else, hmm?"

She knew the flood of heat to her face gave her plans away completely. Rio wrapped an arm around her waist to hug her closely and reached for the last two metro tickets to get them back to the hotel.

"It's time for Daddy to examine a precious work of art he gets to take home tomorrow."

*　*　*

RIO LEANED against the seatback on the plane with his arm around his Little girl. He couldn't believe how much had happened in such a short amount of time. Tenderly, he brushed back a lock of hair that had fallen over her face.

"Daddy?" she whispered at his touch.

"Go back to sleep, Ella. Daddy's got you."

She clutched the green stuffie a bit tighter to her chest and tumbled back into sleep. Amber had worried about having Limey out of her carryon during the flight but had struggled to fall asleep without him. With Limey tucked under the light airplane blanket, she'd relaxed enough to sleep.

Using one hand, Rio accessed the plane's Wi-Fi and checked his messages. Finding an urgent message, he read the contents carefully before easing his arm from around Amber to pull his computer from his case. He was deep into a stack of spreadsheets when she woke and looked around.

Immediately, she carefully tucked Limey back into her bag and looked around to see if anyone had noticed.

"You're okay, Ella. Did you have a nice nap?"

"You're working?" she asked and grimaced at the thought. "I guess we can't stay on vacation all the time."

"You'd miss nursing," he guessed.

"Most days, I'd agree. Others…" She allowed her voice to trail off before looking past him into the aisle. "I think I need to go to the bathroom."

Rio quickly marked his spot and jotted a few notes. With that done, he closed his computer. Before standing to let her scoot past, Rio leaned over and instructed, "Take your panties off, Little girl, and bring them to me."

She looked at him in astonishment before hissing, "I can't sit on the plane without underwear on."

"You can." Rio stood and stepped out of the row.

"I'm not going to do that," she muttered at him as she passed.

"Guidelines," Rio reminded her.

He watched as she shook her head no the entire trip up the aisle. She turned to meet his gaze at the door. When he nodded, she darted into the small airplane restroom.

Watching her settle into her role as a Little girl enchanted him. Change was always hard, but for someone who had hidden that Little girl inside herself for twenty years, it was a challenge. Rio would never push her past her limits, but he definitely intended to challenge Amber. She needed to learn to accept his authority.

A small line formed outside the bathrooms as he waited for her to return. When the door finally opened, Amber dodged the other passengers in the aisle to return to him. She did not meet his gaze.

Without a word, Rio stood and allowed her to scoot past him into the window seat. Immediately, Amber pulled her skirt down as far as possible and pulled the blanket over her lap and chest.

"Let me help you with your seatbelt, Ella." Rio leaned under the blanket to find the two ends and connect them fully.

He placed one hand on her thigh under the cover and met her gaze. "Are you a good girl, Amber?"

"Yes," she whispered. "This is ridiculous, Rio. You don't have to tell me to do something just to prove you're the one in charge."

"You assume incorrectly that this was just a power move." He held his hand out.

Seconds passed before she reached under the blanket and tugged a small scrap of material from her pocket. Wadding it up, she placed it in his hand.

"Thank you, Little girl." Casually, he lifted it to his nose as if he were covering a yawn and inhaled.

"Daddy!" she protested softly and slumped back against the seat when he relented and tucked the small garment into his laptop case. "Hey. Give those back. I'll go put them back on in a few minutes."

"You've lost the privilege of wearing panties for twenty-four hours."

"Would you like anything to drink?" their flight attendant spoke from beside them.

"Ella?" he asked as if she hadn't interrupted anything.

"Can I have a diet cola, please?"

"Of course. And you, sir?"

"Ice water, please."

When she moved on to take the next row's orders, Rio sat his laptop case on his lap and opened a pocket. Palming a small oval-shaped item, he turned slightly in his seat and blocked the view of his motions with the large computer bag on his lap. Before she could guess his intentions, he slid his hand under the blanket and pulled the hem of her skirt up.

"Spread your legs, sweetheart."

"Rio. No! Stop whatever you're doing."

He didn't move but waited for her to follow his directions as he counted, "One, two, three…"

"What are you doing?" she pleaded.

"I'm counting the number of minutes this device in my hand will stay on." He pressed it against her soft mound and activated the controller.

Vibrations instantly assailed her. Even at this location, he knew she could feel the effect on her body. "Eight, nine, ten."

Staring at him in horror, she separated her legs. Immediately, he tucked the small vibrator into her pink folds against her sensitive clit. With regret, Rio removed his hand from the shielding blanket.

"Ten minutes," he reminded her as he removed his laptop from his case to continue working. Moving deliberately, he created a timer display on the screen and set it to ten minutes. He opened his spreadsheets and resumed working. A few minutes later, he pressed the button on the small controller in his hand as he started the countdown.

Amber's fingers clenched together on her lap as her gaze crashed into his. "No."

"Don't tell Daddy no." Rio set the timer back to ten minutes and restarted it.

"Thirty seconds had already elapsed," she protested, wiggling to get away from the vibration.

"Be good. I can always add time. Sit still. I could hold it in place if you'd prefer."

Instantly, she shook her head no and tried to relax back against the seat.

Paying attention to her body language, Rio watched her squeeze her legs together and grip her fingers on the armrest next to her. He clicked on a document to cover the timer from her view and scanned the next problematic financial document as he made electronic notes.

When Amber stiffened in her chair, he turned off the device and stopped the timer before meeting her shocked gaze. "I was almost…"

"Here's your diet cola and your water."

They each accepted the glasses and a snack before the flight attendant moved on.

Amber lifted the plastic cup to her mouth and drank deeply. After lowering her tray, she set the glass down with a definite thud as she sent Rio a disgruntled look.

Rio selected the timer once again and reset it for ten minutes, replacing the two minutes she'd already experienced.

"Stop that."

"We have several hours left on this flight. These ten minutes could stretch out to a long time."

With a huff, she turned to look out the window. When several minutes passed and he didn't turn the vibrator back on, she leaned close and asked, "What are you waiting for?"

"You haven't learned yet who's in charge. When you do, I'll reward you with ten minutes of pleasure."

He watched her peeved expression disappear from her face as Amber processed his words. It was up to her to decide if this was a punishment or a reward.

She sat quietly for a few more minutes as she finished her soda. When the flight attendant collected their empty cups, Amber carefully wiped any remnant of liquid from her tray before pulling her coloring book and pencils from her carryon. After a sideways glance at his computer screen, she chose a color and opened the book to a random page to begin decorating it.

Rio arranged his open documents so that the timer appeared in the corner of his screen. "Lift your pencil, Little girl."

"What?" she asked, raising the red one in her hand as she turned to look at him.

Triggering the device and the timer, Rio leaned over to cup her face and kiss her lightly. He adjusted the blanket over her, casually brushing his fingertips across her erect nipples. A small gasp escaped from her lips at his caress.

Thanking the normal engine noise that covered the quiet hum between her legs and the small noises she tried to contain, Rio pressed his lips to her throat before whispering into her ear, "Who's in charge, Little girl?"

"Daddy."

"What does that mean?"

"Daddy gets to make the rules."

"Why?" Rio pushed her to put all the pieces together.

After a few seconds, she answered, "Because he knows what I need."

"What do you need right now, Ella?"

"I don't know."

"I don't think that's the truth. No panties for you tomorrow." He increased the speed of the hum between her legs.

"I need to come," she answered quickly.

"Does this help?" he asked, turning the device on and off to make the vibration almost jump between her legs.

"I don't think it's in the right place. I wiggled too much."

"Hmm, what should we do about that?" he asked, smoothing out the vibration to a steady hum.

"Can you fix it?" Amber quickly tucked her pencil back in the case and closed her coloring book before easing her thighs apart to make way for his touch.

Turning his computer so the screen blocked the view of those across the aisle, Rio reached under the blanket and into the wetness that had gathered between her legs. Readjusting the vibrating device, he deliberately brushed over her clit several times. Her moan clued him in to the most effective placement. After tapping it several times, he removed his hand. With a pat to her thigh, he returned to his spreadsheets.

Trying to notice anything suspicious in the mass of numbers was challenging on a regular day, but with his Little girl doing her best to stay quiet and not attract attention, it was impossible. Rio adjusted the inseam of his pants. Thank goodness for the tray table that provided some cover.

When Amber tensed in her chair, Rio lowered the vibration to the lowest setting. Two more minutes remained on the timer.

"What happens in two minutes?" the flight attendant asked, pausing in her rounds down the aisle to pick up trash.

"I get to stop pretending I'm working," Rio said with a laugh.

"I won't tell if you shut everything down now," she teased, flirting with him.

"Unfortunately, when using a work-assigned computer, they can track how efficient you've been. If you'll excuse me?" he asked, before focusing back on the data in front of him.

"That's awful. There's something tracking everyone these days," she groused but continued toward the front of plane.

Thirty seconds left. He cranked the vibration up and watched Amber bite her lip as she fell apart. Her hand slid over his forearm to grip his hand. Rio understood immediately that she needed a connection with him.

When the digital timer expired, he turned off the vibration. The expression on her face made him lean sideways to whisper, "I wish I could hold you in my lap, Ella."

"I'd like that so much. When we get off the plane?" she asked.

"Yes, sweetheart. The first chance we can. For now, Daddy's going to take care of you."

In a few seconds, he had his computer put away and his tray stowed. Rio grabbed a few tissues from his bag and crumpled them in his hand. Forcing himself not to linger, Rio reached under the blanket to remove the device and absorb some of the slick juices coating her skin.

"Can I go to the bathroom, Daddy?" she whispered a few minutes later when he had stowed everything away.

"Let me recover a bit first, Ella," he requested as he counted backward from a hundred. Her giggle didn't help his situation.

CHAPTER 17

Clinging to Rio's hand, Amber followed him through the skywalk into the airport. Despite two naps, she was absolutely exhausted. Rio had corralled both their carry-ons and handled everything for her.

At the first opportunity, he led her to an empty area and took a seat, cuddling her on his lap. She smiled against his chest as his hand swept over her thighs, making sure her skirt covered her completely. Even this tired after her first transoceanic flight, Amber had to admit to herself it felt naughty to not wear panties in public.

"Don't we have to go get our luggage?" she asked, wishing she could just stay where she was for a long time.

"Eventually. It will take a few minutes for them to unload the plane. We'll head to baggage claim in a few minutes."

"Ten?" she teased.

"Ten minutes can seem like forever, can't they? You'll remember to listen to me next time, won't you?"

"Yes," she admitted, knowing his ingenuity would always come up with some way to make sure she paid attention.

"I love you, Little girl," he whispered to her.

Tears filled Amber's eyes and she leaned back to look at his face. "Really? I've loved you forever."

"I will never lie to you, Amber. My heart belongs to a beautiful, fiery redhead."

Amber wiped under her eyes, sure her makeup was completely gone after the hours-long trip. "I can't look too wonderful now," she protested.

"My beautiful Little girl," he corrected her. "Would you like to go home?"

"Please."

"Let's go."

In a flash, Rio had their luggage and allowed Amber to only roll one small bag to the parking lot where their car waited. He tucked her in the car despite her protests she could help while he stowed the bags in the trunk. Closing her eyes to rest, she crashed into sleep.

"Wake up, Little girl. We're home," Rio urged.

Operating on automatic, Amber allowed him to steer her into the house. Within minutes, she stood under a warm spray of water as he spread creamy body wash over her skin. She loved feeling all the stress of traveling sliding off to disappear down the drain.

She dipped her head under the water to wet her hair. When she reached for the shampoo, he took it from her to squeeze a small amount onto his hand. Amber moaned as he worked the cleansing foam through her hair and scratched softly across her scalp.

"You can do that forever," she mumbled.

"I think we'll run out of hot water in twenty minutes or so," he teased, tilting her head back under the water to rinse her tresses free of the suds.

"You could have used a cold shower before," she reminded him sleepily.

"You, my teasing Little girl, are absolutely right. Unfortunately, my problem was not as easily handled as yours," he answered, wrapping her in a thick towel before capturing her wet hair in another.

"Do we need to dry your hair before you climb in bed?" he asked, lathering his skin quickly as she lounged against the wall of the large walk-in shower.

"No, Daddy. That makes it frizzy. I do need Limey."

"I'll get him for you."

"Thank you, Daddy. Could you make sure our picture is okay?" She'd stowed the tube very carefully in their luggage so it didn't get damaged.

"Yes, sweetheart," he assured her as he wrapped a towel around his waist.

When he'd smoothed all the moisture from her skin, Rio guided her into the bedroom. Finding Limey in her bag, he tucked the stuffie in her arms and helped her climb into bed. Her Daddy smoothed the crisp sheets and soft comforter around her and kissed her softly.

"Sleep tight, Amberella."

"You'll come to bed soon?" she pleaded.

"Very soon."

"Night, Daddy. Thank you for taking me to Paris and showing me so many things. You'll make my playroom a Monet again, won't you? In the new house?"

"Of course." He kissed her forehead.

When he slid into bed a little later, Amber rolled to lie against his chest. With his arms wrapped around her, she whispered, "I love you, Daddy."

His embrace tightened around her. "I love you, Amber."

*　*　*

"No! Stop!" Amber thrashed to get away from the thousands of arms that held her from running away. They were dragging her into the depths of an endless hole she knew she'd never be able to escape from.

"Ella, sweetheart. You're dreaming. Try to wake up."

The familiar voice sounded so far away. She couldn't lose Rio again. Renewing her struggle to free herself, Amber kicked the bonds wrapped around her feet. She was suffocating in the heat that surrounded her. "Daddy!"

"I'm here, Little girl. Let me help you," he urged.

Amber could feel the air beginning to cool around her. Still, something held her feet in place. She'd never be able to reach Rio.

"I've got you, Ella," Rio assured her. His hand swept down her side to loosen the hold on her legs. "How did you get so tangled? Concentrate on my voice, Amber. Try to wake up."

"Daddy?" she whispered, trying to reach him. Her eyes blinked open to see him leaning over her, tugging the covers away. "You saved me."

"That was some dream, Little girl. You tangled yourself in the sheets so tightly."

"The sheets? I thought they were arms dragging me away from you."

"Nothing can steal you away, Ella. I plan to always be here to save you," he promised.

With her eyes open, Amber succeeded in freeing herself from the swath of material around her torso. Instantly, she threw herself forward to wrap her arms around his neck, peppering his face with kisses.

Muscles bulging, he pulled her out of the confining web around her legs and into his lap. Rio held her close, rocking her gently. "Want to tell Daddy about your dream?"

"It was awful. There were all these hands pulling me down into a big dark abyss. I knew I'd never get out again."

"That sounds very scary," he comforted her, running a hand through her hair.

"My heart was pounding."

"You gave mine a workout, too."

"I'm sorry I woke you up. Go back to sleep," she urged, feeling guilty.

"Never worry about waking me up, Little girl. If you have a bad dream, that's exactly what you should do. How can I frighten away anything that messes with you if you don't tell me?"

That totally made sense to her still sleep-addled brain. Nodding her agreement, she laid her head on his shoulder and tried to push all the dark thoughts from her mind. Nothing would get her in his arms.

He held her quietly for several minutes as her body and mind calmed. When she raised her head to press a grateful kiss to his lips, Rio hugged her tight.

"Better?"

"Yes, Daddy. Wow! I made a mess of the bed."

"Go potty and I'll straighten everything. I think Limey ran away."

"Oh, no!" Amber scrambled from the bed to drop to her knees on the carpet. She searched around in the darkness on the floor for the stuffie. "I can't find him. He didn't get sucked into the void, did he?"

"We'll find Limey. He'd never stray too far from you," Rio assured her as he slid out of bed.

After turning on the bedside lamp, he spotted a bit of green plush. "Here he is. Limey was hiding under your pillow."

"That's a good spot," Amber celebrated, scrambling up from the floor. "It's really dark in here without the light. Limey might be a bit afraid at night."

"Hmm. We can't have Limey frightened by the dark, can we? I'll get a nightlight in the morning."

"Thanks, Daddy."

"Go potty," he reminded her.

"Oops!" Suddenly, she really needed to use the bathroom.

When she returned, Rio was stretching the covers back over her side of the bed. "Perfect timing."

She hesitated next to the bed and scooped Limey up in her arms. "Could we sleep in my playroom for the rest of the night?"

"Nothing is going to get you while you sleep now, Little girl."

"I know, but…could we?"

"Of course." Rio took her hand and led her to the beautiful room. He turned on a small lamp next to the twin bed pushed against the wall and folded back the sheet. "In you go. Daddy will sleep on the outside to protect you."

Scrambling into bed, Amber scootched to the far side to give Rio as much room as possible. When he wrapped himself around her, Amber relaxed against his hard frame.

The early morning light shone through the window when her eyes blinked open next. Rio's hands brushed over her skin as he nibbled a devastating path down her neck. She wiggled against him and froze at the feel of his thick shaft pressing against her bottom.

Rio pressed her knee higher and stroked down her thigh. His light touch sent shivers through her, stoking the fire that his kisses had kindled.

"You're wet, Ella. Would you like Daddy to make love to you?" he whispered against her ear as his fingers traced the cleft of her pussy and dipped inside to caress her intimately.

"Please," she breathed.

Amber tried to roll over to face him, but Rio kept her tethered in place. "Daddy!" she protested as one finger pressed into her tight channel.

"Daddy's in charge."

Exploring her body, Rio returned to the sensitive places he had memorized. His touch made her want more. So much more.

Reaching one arm around him, she trailed her hand along his toned body. The position he kept her in didn't allow her to play very much. "I want to touch you, too," she begged, turning her head to look at him as much as possible.

"It will be your playtime later. Now it's Daddy's turn," he promised. Lifting his hand from between her thighs, Rio brought his fingers to his mouth and slowly licked her shiny juices away.

"Mmm!"

The fire within her flamed higher as she watched him. She wiggled against his body, drawing a groan from him. When he turned to grab a condom from the bedside table, Amber tried to turn over, but he maintained his hold on her.

Within seconds, he pressed his cock to her entrance and lifted her leg over his hard thigh. Rio pushed slowly inside, filling her completely as his body surrounded her.

"Mine, Little girl. You belong to me," he claimed her, running his hand over her breasts to tease her nipples.

"Yours." She wiggled against him.

Amber didn't know what turned her on more: Rio's physical dominance or his possession. When he started moving, she decided she didn't care. Turning Limey to face the wall, she abandoned herself to the passion and her Daddy's control.

CHAPTER 18

Walking into the hospital for her first day of work, Amber carried a nutritious lunch and some unhealthy snacks to get her through the twelve-hour shift. The emergency department was hopping with patients with a wide variety of ailments. Amber dove into work with the experienced team.

"Code Triage," sounded on the intercom, warning of a large influx of patients who were on their way to the hospital from an accident.

"What happened? Does anyone know?" Amber asked.

"A gunman tried to rob a bar downtown," an orderly reported.

"Which one?"

"Murphy's."

Amber stopped to look at him in shock. "Murphy's? That's my dad's bar. I mean Rio's bar."

"A bunch of injuries ranging in severity are coming in."

"Do you know their names?"

"No. They're not reporting that."

Her mind whirling, Amber pulled out her phone with shaking hands to call Rio. The message went straight to voicemail. She tried to control her pounding heart as she listened to his deep voice. "Rio, I need you to call me now and tell me you're okay. There was a shooting at Murphy's."

"Are you okay to work?" the emergency department director asked, pinning her with his assessing gaze.

"I'm okay. It's better to help than to worry," she assured him, trying to pull it together. Everyone would be brought here. If Rio was hurt, she'd know faster than if she drove like a crazy woman around town trying to find him.

"The first patients are coming now. Take the first bay."

"Yes, sir."

Glad to have something to focus on, Amber hurried to meet the paramedics at the door to the first treatment room. They ran through the patient's statistics and injuries as they wheeled in a familiar face.

"Jeri? I'm Amber. We met at Murphy's a few weeks ago. I'm going to get you set up here for treatment. Are you in any pain?"

"Amber. I remember you."

"Are you in pain?" Amber repeated as the paramedics transferred her to the bed.

"No. They gave me good drugs," the server admitted to Amber.

"Perfect."

"Rio pushed me out of the way. He saved a bunch of people," Jeri told her.

"Is he okay?" Amber asked as she did her job on autopilot, helping get Jeri moved over onto the hospital bed and hanging up the IV line they'd already started.

"Hello. I hear you have a shoulder I need to take care of." The doctor interrupted Jeri from answering as he walked in the door.

Amber decided that Jeri was her best friend when the server looked around the surgeon to meet her gaze. "He made them take me first to the hospital."

Digesting all the information in that statement, Amber knew Rio was injured and would be coming to the hospital. She also knew that he was coherent enough to be bossy. Trying to focus on the positive, she arranged for the X-rays the doctor requested.

At her first free moment, Amber peeked into the other treatment rooms. No Rio. *Please let him be okay.* She needed him to be okay.

The organized chaos in the emergency department flowed like a choreographed ballet. Even sick with worry about Rio, she knew this was a good place for him to come get the best care. Ambulances streamed in with patients. She was pleased to see a few discharged after initial treatment.

"The last patients are on their way in," the director shared as Amber darted into a bay to assist a doctor in stitching up a wound.

He had to be okay. She kept reminding herself they would have insisted on bringing him in first if he was critical. A colleague called her name at the door of a bay and Amber rushed toward her.

"Rio?" she asked.

"He's asking for you. Come in and let him see you so we can treat him."

"Rio!" Amber said, darting through the privacy curtain.

"Ella," he answered. "I'd give you a hug, but I don't want to get you messy."

"What happened to you?" Amber asked, searching over his body. Blood was splattered over his chest and arms, but she didn't find any wounds.

"Damn broken leg."

"You broke your leg?"

"She found you before I could find her," the paramedic observed, coming back into the room to fist bump Rio.

The new arrival looked at Amber to say, "This guy owes me a few dozen beers. He refused to let me take him to the hospital until we'd taken care of everyone else."

"It's just a leg," Rio explained when Amber looked at him. "You're ratting me out, Nelson."

"According to the crowd, there would have been many more injured if not for this guy, pushing people behind the bar for safety and then vaulting over it to tackle the assailant," the paramedic shared.

"They're exaggerating." Rio brushed away the accolades.

Amber knew they weren't. She gave him her best mad nurse look before scanning his lower body this time. Everything looked okay except one foot pointed the wrong way.

"Ouch," she commiserated.

"I'd say surgery is in your future," Nelson projected.

"I guess you don't need me here," the doctor joked as he walked into the room. "I'll just thank the man of the hour here for preventing more injuries."

"Dr. Urial, this is Rio. He's my…" Amber searched for a word to let the doctor know what Rio meant to her. "He's my everything. Can you patch him back up?"

"I can with a visit to the operating room," Dr. Urial assured them. "I've looked at the X-rays. It looks like you'll need a plate and some screws to fortify that break so it can heal properly."

Amber ran her fingers through his hair when Rio flopped his head back against the pillows. She knew he was beating himself up for letting himself get hurt.

"We'll wait until the morning when we're both fresh to get that taken care of and the trauma surgeons have finished all the gun wound injuries. We'll keep your pain down as much as possible in the meantime."

"Thank you, Doctor," Amber said gratefully as she clung to Rio's hand.

"I'll take a look now and double check what I saw on the X-rays."

After Dr. Urial's exam, Amber could tell that Rio was in pain. She rang quickly for his nurse. When the emergency department director entered the bay, he asked Amber to step outside the cubicle.

"It's against policy for you to take care of a relative in your capacity as a nurse. Want to clock out for lunch and get him cleaned up off duty?"

Amber smiled at the stern-faced man. He didn't know her at all as this was her first day working at the hospital. He could have ordered her back to work with a warning or canned her when she insisted on taking care of Rio.

"Thank you, sir. I'll clock out and get him set to go up to the floor when they have a room for him. I won't interfere with his nurse. Promise."

"I'll hold you to it. You have thirty minutes. Make the most of it. If we have another rush of injuries, you'll have to cut your lunch short."

"Yes, sir." Amber turned to jog through the department, dodging machinery, healthcare workers, and patients. She checked herself out for lunch and returned in a flash to gather a small tub and washcloths, along with a few other items.

The look Rio gave her as she walked in made her heart flutter in her chest. He was as glad to see her as she was to see him. She could have lost him. Amber vowed to treasure every moment they had together.

"Did you get more pain medicine?" she asked.

"Yes, Nurse Murphy."

"You." Amber waggled her finger at him. "Now, I'm in charge, Rio." She turned on the faucet to warm the water.

"Maybe until they get me put back together again," he allowed.

"And you're back on your feet."

"We'll see about that."

"This T-shirt is toast," she told him, cutting the deep pink material off with a pair of shears in seconds.

"Do you all take lessons on cutting clothes off people?" he asked, lifting the sheet to show her his thigh and hip. "Nelson ruined my favorite pair of jeans."

"You should be glad he didn't try to take them off the normal way. And, yes, we take all sorts of classes. I'm sure Nelson's a pro. I'll bring you some shorts to wear home. I'm going to get to check out your legs for a while," she joked as she carried the basin over to the bedside table and dipped a cloth into the warm water.

Carefully, she washed his face, arms, and torso. "You were too close to danger, Daddy," she whispered after making sure they were alone.

"I'm sorry I scared you, Amberella."

"I'm just glad you're okay. I love you."

"I love you, too."

In a few minutes, she had him settled comfortably in a clean gown. She'd even washed his hair with a shampoo cap. From the number of nurses that stopped by to offer to help, Amber knew her handsome man would receive a lot of attention while he was in the hospital. He was definitely not the typical patient filling the hospital bed. Even in pain with a broken leg, Rio was drop-dead gorgeous.

"I'm going to have to get you a stick to beat off all the people who want to help you. Just don't let them give you five sponge baths a day. It's not good for your skin," she teased.

"No one's giving me a sponge bath but you," he growled.

"Let the nurses take care of you, Rio. That's what they're here for," she assured him.

Catching sight of the time, she brushed her fingers through his damp hair. "I have to go back to work. They'll have a room for you soon. I'll come see you at the end of my shift," she told him.

"Go home and sleep," he ordered.

"Maybe after I see you."

Dragging herself away, Amber retraced her steps to the time clock and logged back into work. The next time she had a break to stop by his room, a teenage girl getting an asthma treatment lay on the bed. Amber waved hello and excused herself to find out what room Rio was in. With the number noted in her phone, she met Nelson and his partner at the door with a new patient.

CHAPTER 19

"You should be at home, Little girl," he mumbled.

"Like that's going to happen with you here," she answered, wiping his lips with a damp cloth. "I always have an extra pair of scrubs in my trunk, and I used your shower while you were sleeping. They'll make do with me minus makeup today."

"You look beautiful just as you are," he said and shifted in the bed, making them both wince.

She knew the pain that had to cause. "They're going to take you to surgery this morning first thing. I've checked out your doctor with the nurses and everyone says Dr. Urial is the best."

"Thank you," the doctor said on cue as he walked into the room.

"Hi, Doc," Rio greeted him with a smile.

"Ready to get this leg straightened back up? Any questions?"

"What's the prognosis after it heals?"

"You seem fit and active. I'll know more when I see your bone density, but I suspect you'll heal well, and most people will never suspect you were ever injured."

"But I'll know, huh? It's not going to be the same?" Rio asked.

"I'll order therapy. It looks like you already have your own nurse to make sure you take it easy and heal before running a marathon," the doctor tried to reassure him. "I think we'll have a good result. You might discover you can feel when the weather is changing or some other miscellaneous effects."

"Thank you, Doctor, for taking care of Rio. He's pretty special to me. We just got back together after twenty years apart."

"Then I better get you back in shape so you can dance at your wedding," the kind doctor suggested on his way out with a wave.

"I've already seen your moves," Amber teased, remembering dancing with him at the reunion.

"Yeah, I need to be able to do that, too," Rio answered with a wink.

"Dancing moves," she corrected with a laugh before leaning in to whisper, "Those other ones, too. I like them a lot."

"They're ready for you downstairs," a nurse announced from the doorway. "Transport is on his way to get you. I'm going to give you some pain meds before they rattle you along the floor."

"Thank you," Amber rushed to say as she moved away from his IV tubing.

"It's definitely what I'd want someone to do for me," the nurse answered and injected the liquid into his line. The two nurses watched Rio's face relax before she patted his tattooed forearm. "I'll see you back here in a few hours."

"Could you let me know when he's back?" Amber asked. "I'll be working in the emergency department."

"Definitely." She looked at the information board on the wall where Amber had noted her name and number as the contact person for his care. "Are you Amber?"

"That's me."

"I'll let you know when I have him settled."

"Thank you."

* * *

AMBER ATE breakfast in the cafeteria before clocking in for her shift. She kept an eye on the clock to judge how the surgery was going.

When her phone rang three hours after she'd kissed him for good luck, Amber breathed a sigh of relief.

Knowing he'd sleep for a while, she delayed taking her lunch. When she got to his room, Rio's luxurious eyelashes lay against his skin. Trying to be quiet, she looked over all his vitals with a practiced eye.

"Hi," he rasped.

"Hi. Have a sip of water. That will help your throat," she encouraged, holding the straw to his lips.

"Ahh! That's good. Thank you. Is it all done?"

"I'm assuming so. You've got a big bandage on your leg and a non-weight bearing sign on your wall."

"That's going to suck."

"You'll need some help to negotiate for a while. We'll figure it out," she assured him.

"Yes. Can I eat? I'm starving," Rio asked, pulling himself up in bed and wincing at the pain.

"Slow movements are going to be your friend," she advised. "What sounds good?"

"I heard you rustling around in here and brought you some sherbet and sunflower butter crackers," a nurse's aide said cheerfully as she walked in.

Catching her first glimpse of Rio awake, she blurted, "You are as good looking as everyone said."

Amber couldn't help laughing at the young woman's words. She didn't dare look at Rio. If they both started laughing, Rio would jostle himself badly in bed. "He is."

"And taken, I guess," the aide said, opening the small container of rainbow sherbet.

"Completely," Rio answered. "Thank you. Rainbow is my favorite sherbet flavor."

"Crap! And you even have good taste," the aide joked. "I'm Stephanie. Need anything else?"

When Rio shook his head, Stephanie added a plastic container with a lid. "This is a urinal to use here until they clear you to get up with help. Therapy will be here later. Press the button if you need help. I'll be back with fresh ice and water."

"Thank you, Stephanie," Rio answered politely.

After she left, Rio asked, "Please tell me I can use that thing myself."

"Eventually. You're probably a bit groggy now. Let me help you." Pulling the privacy curtain, she helped him use the device and righted his gown and sheet.

"Thank you," he said gratefully.

"We'll play nurse and naughty patient when we get you home," Amber teased as she washed her hands.

"Naughty nurse and recovering patient, maybe," he corrected her with a stern look.

"Eat your sherbet. I'll see you after my shift is over."

"Go home. Sleep in our bed."

"I'm off tomorrow. We'll sleep together."

"This is not the place to put ideas into my head," he growled softly when she leaned close to kiss him.

* * *

"Thank goodness it's my left foot so I can drive," Rio groused.

She knew he was feeling better when he started chafing at the restrictions his injury caused. "Want to go to Murphy's for dinner tonight?" she suggested casually. "I know everyone would love to see you."

"There better not be any jolly good hero celebration planned," he stated firmly.

For days, the front gate of the neighborhood had been inundated with reporters trying to get to Rio's house to interview him. The guard shack was now filled with cookies and snack mixes Rio had sent them as an apology. In response, Charlie had replied with a photo of him signing Rio's name and a sign offering to see the hero's signature for five bucks each. They were definitely blessed that everyone inconvenienced by the mob didn't complain too loudly.

"No jolly good celebrations. Promise." Amber crossed her heart.

"In that case, I'd love to devour one of their giant pretzels and a beer."

"Had any pain killers lately?" she asked.

"No, Nurse Amber. Just over the counter tablets."

Amber brought him the crutches Rio insisted on using. She insisted on driving, of course, and wouldn't argue with him drinking one beer if he hadn't taken the prescription pain killers. As they approached Murphy's, she could see the parking lot was full. By luck, she found a space close to the door.

"You're going to be able to pay Dr. Urial's bill," she joked, opening the door for him.

Rio got two hops inside the door before everyone yelled, "Surprise!"

"You are so spanked," he growled at her quietly.

"You have to catch me first," she answered with a smile before adding, "It's as much for them as it is for you."

She watched Rio scan the crowd as people started to swarm forward. "Let's get Rio a chair," she suggested as she led him through the crowd to an empty seat.

In clumps and alone, people came up to speak to Rio. She could tell he didn't like the spotlight but was glad to see everyone. Amber didn't care when even Jeri hugged him, especially when she hugged Amber first.

"I'm glad to see you're okay," Rio told her.

"Thanks, Rio. I'm back at work but someone always carries my tray for me. It was hard to walk in that first night, but Murphy's welcomed me back," Jeri assured him.

Soon the rush of people to greet and thank Rio slowed down. He got his big pretzel with beer cheese with a burger on the side that Amber helped him eat. Harper and Colt settled into chairs at their table and Rio looked around, waiting for the mob to come for Colt.

"I'm old news around here now," Colt said, noting Rio's scan of the room.

"Good. It's time for life to go back to normal," Rio announced.

Amber tried to figure out what was going on with her friends. Colt sat close to Harper, but her girlfriend sent off waves of apprehension. Something was up. Were they together or not?

Before she could ask any questions, Amber's phone rang with a video call. "Maisie? Where are you?"

"Washington. Sorry I can't be there. Tell Rio I'm glad he and the bar are okay."

"Here. Talk to him yourself." Amber passed the phone over.

"Sparky?"

She stood and whirled to see her parents standing behind her. Everything had been so crazy, she hadn't seen them since they'd gotten back from the cruise. Amber stood and threw her arms around her dad's neck to hug him before moving on to embrace her mom.

She saw Rio end the phone call and wave to catch the nearest bartender's attention. To her delight, the young man rang a brass bell she hadn't noticed before and announced, "Murphy in the establishment!"

Cheers of "Murphy!" filled the air as longtime patrons greeted the former owner. Amber could see how touched her dad was and her mom's eyes teared up.

As Jack Murphy stepped forward to shake Rio's hand, Gretchen Murphy whispered to her daughter, "He was a bit nervous to come tonight. I think it bothered him not to be the guy in charge that everyone wants to talk to after so many years. That was very nice of your fellow."

"Rio's an amazing guy. He always was."

"So, you two are serious?" her mom probed.

"Yes. He's building a house for us, and we'll get married eventually," Amber shared.

"You'll let me help plan the wedding?"

"I wouldn't want anyone else's guidance. It won't be anything big," Amber warned, not wanting her mom to get too crazy.

"It's your wedding."

Amber turned at the sound of her phone ringing again. Rio

answered the second video call of the night and began chatting with Beau.

Something clicked in Amber's mind. "Excuse me, Mom. I'll say something to Beau quickly. Come sit with us," she urged as she moved to look over Rio's shoulder.

"Hi, Beau!"

"Hi, Amber. Just checking in on Rio. Sorry I'm missing the party. I should be back in town soon," Beau reported. "Shoot. I have to go. See you soon."

Amber met Rio's gaze and asked, "Did you notice that was the same couch?"

"The same couch?" Rio echoed.

"He was sitting on the same couch as Maisie was. Did he sweet talk her into letting him stay at her house?" Amber grinned as she considered what that could mean.

"There are a lot of beige couches in the world, Amber," Rio warned.

"Not with those pillows. It was like a mirror image of the pattern but in opposite colors."

Rio just shook his head and carefully stood to greet her parents. "Jack and Mrs. Murphy. I'm glad to see you."

"You've made a few changes in here. It looks good. Does that freezer still leak?" Jack asked, leaning in confidentially.

"No, sir. That was the first thing I replaced. The repair guy couldn't believe it was still working," Rio reported.

"I babied that freezer for years," Jack said with a laugh before sobering. "So, you and my daughter?"

"Yes, we're together."

"There was always something between the two of you—an undeniable friendship."

"I love Amber, Jack. I plan to take very good care of her."

Jack looked at Amber. "You love him?"

"I do. Now that we're together, nothing will pull us apart again," Amber said, warning her father that she was a grown woman now who would make up her own mind.

"Good. I like happy endings," her father shared, shocking her.

Amber watched her father hold out his hand to Rio and welcome him to the family. She looked at her mother in surprise.

"He always liked Rio. Your father was afraid you'd miss your chance to get out of this town and see the world. Teenage romances rarely last for long. Maybe he was wrong to try to keep you apart. I guess we'll never know. We're both glad you're happy now," her mom confessed.

Amber felt Rio's arm wrap around her waist and hug her to his body. She tried not to lean on him but he held her flush against him.

"I couldn't be happier, Mom."

"Let me buy you a beer, Jack," Rio said, signaling the server.

"I'd like that, Rio."

Amber knew this would have never happened twenty years ago. She smiled at her mother who nodded and winked. Amber knew who'd gotten her dad there.

CHAPTER 20

Rio walked slowly over the uneven ground to check out the footings of their future house together. He leaned on Amber a bit from time to time and knew it wouldn't be long before he scooped her up in his arms to carry her over the threshold. The amount of milk his Little girl had him drink every day had to make his bones heal even stronger than before.

"So, what's the plan for the driveway?" she asked, staring at the small creek that ran in front of the house.

"Good question. We can put in a bridge or just let people four-wheel it over the rocks. That will keep people away," he projected.

"Daddy. We want people to come visit. My car won't want to roll over those boulders back there," Amber said, worrying her bottom lip with her teeth.

"A bridge it is, then. I plan to put a sensor on it to let us know when someone crosses it," Rio told her.

"Why?"

"That new idea from the builder to suspend a daybed outside made me realize we'll need a warning system."

"You have plans?" she asked with a smirk.

"The doctor said I'd need more rest while I'm healing. A nap will do your Daddy good, too."

"He said that weeks ago, Rio. And I don't think you're talking about napping," she pointed out.

"No arguing with your elders, Little girl," he reminded her with a firm pat to her bottom.

"Ouch!" she exclaimed and shimmied away. "You have a hard hand."

She'd gotten by with being bossy while he recovered. Last night, Rio had put an end to that. Amber needed to go back to being his Little girl and not the nurse when she was off duty. The tiny lines had evaporated from her face this morning. He'd known she wasn't sleeping well. A hot bottom and multiple orgasms had tired her out last night. He'd made a note of that prescription for good sleep.

"I'll make sure you remember," he warned.

Instead of rolling her eyes and grouching about his punishment, Amber slid her hand into his. "I'm glad you're better."

"Me, too. My bike has been lonely without me."

"Daddy!"

"Just kidding, Little girl. You're much more important than the ability to shift gears on my bike."

Rio was quiet for a few seconds before studying her face. "Can I tell you a secret? You won't be able to share it."

"Of course."

"Colt confided that he bought the parcel of land next to us."

"No way! Wait until I talk to Harper."

"Ella," he said in a low warning.

"She doesn't know?"

"No. It's his secret to share. Can you be good?" Rio asked with a stern glint in his eyes.

"I'll be good," she promised before rising on her toes to scan the horizon. "Can we see where he'll build?"

"Not from here, Ella. I think he'll put his house closer to the main road than we did. I'd bet Colt has a plan for that front corner that's closest to town."

"We need to have them over for dinner or something," she proposed.

"Don't mess around in your friends' business," Rio warned. "They need to figure this out without interference."

"I wouldn't meddle," she insisted before swallowing hard when he looked at her skeptically. "Okay, I'd meddle, but just a bit."

"Would you have wanted Colt and Harper's help with our relationship?"

"No, but…"

"Harper doesn't know that Colt has purchased the land. Best to let him share the news with her. He told me in confidence," Rio reminded her.

They walked around the perimeter of the house as Rio checked out the work that the crew had begun. He pointed out the different rooms as they checked out how it was coming to life from the house plans they'd perfected.

By the time they got to the footprint for the kitchen, Amber caved. "Okay. You're right. I won't say anything about the land and I'll try not to grill Harper about what's going on until they're ready to discuss it. Can I at least tell her I'm here if she wants to talk?"

Rio looked at the woman by his side. "We waited so long to have each other in our lives. Their path is going to be different than ours. Hopefully, they'll be as happy as we are. They have to find their way together."

"Okay, fine. You're right. I wouldn't have wanted their interference, either, but it's going to be hard," she complained.

"Support your friend but don't meddle, Little girl."

Looking up at his handsome face, Amber knew her expression revealed her struggle to not try to assist her friends. "I'm going to do my best," she promised.

"I'll just have to keep you busy, Ella."

"Busy?" she echoed.

"I thought we might take up a new activity together."

"What's that? Intensive napping?" she accused.

"That doesn't sound bad, but I thought we might want to try scuba diving."

"Where would we go scuba diving?" she asked in total confusion.

"The Galapagos Islands?" he suggested.

"Like the place with the endangered wildlife?" she asked, instantly interested.

"Exactly. I'm going to Quito, Ecuador next month and I thought you might like to go with me."

"Yes! I'd love that. I mean, it isn't Paris… But turtles are better than the Eiffel Tower, right?"

"Don't ask a Frenchman that or we'll never be allowed back in the country," he suggested, laughing.

"I bet there's shots we'll have to get," she commented a few seconds later, obviously having considered the ramification of the trip.

"You give shots every day, sweetheart. You can't be afraid to get one."

"Not everyone is as nice as me. Some people jab them hard. Maybe I don't like turtles anyway," she muttered.

"If I go with you to the doctor's office, would that make you feel better?" Rio asked.

Immediately, she nodded her head. "Yes, Daddy. That would be much better. And…"

"And what?" he asked when her voice trailed away without finishing her statement.

"Maybe we could get ice cream afterward? Or go play mini golf? That would help me forget about the pain," she promised.

"I think we could do one of those things." Rio wasn't going to tell her until the last minute that several shots might be required, depending on what she'd already had to protect her in the emergency department.

"I could probably go with you then. You'd get lonely without me," she informed him.

Rio wrapped his arm around her waist and hugged her close to his side. "I would indeed, Little girl."

EPILOGUE

Harper looked at the vicious woman holding the sweet toddler. Crossing her fingers behind her back, Harper hoped to have some effect on how Cinderella treated others when she got older.

"Miranda, I don't think you need to worry about my love life," she said quietly, hoping that would end the conversation.

"I don't think you qualify as having a love life, Harper. All you do is take care of other people's kids. I worried about you being bright enough to care for Cinderella, but she'll be in school before any lack of mental stimulation puts her behind other students."

"Let me assure you, Miranda, that all the children in my care have a wide variety of experiences and interactions. I've done my research to make sure that everyone learns as much as possible during their time with me. It would help if you would support my efforts. Tomorrow, everyone is bringing something that starts with the letter D. Have a conversation with Cinderella about things that start with a D."

When Miranda looked at her blankly, Harper continued, "You know, dog, doughnut, dime, dinosaur…"

With a hiss of exasperation, Miranda interrupted. "I know what starts with the letter D. I didn't barely make it through high school."

"High school was a long time ago, Miranda."

"I know. That's what brings me back to what I was trying to discuss with you when you rudely shut me down. I'm only trying to help, and Rufus is a good guy, I'm sure."

"I do not wish to go to the reunion with the homeless guy you have living outside your office. While I'm sure you would be happy to have someone take him in from the street so you don't have to worry about him discouraging clients from visiting your knickknack store…"

"Collectibles, Harper!"

"Of course. As I was saying, your collectibles shop…"

"I don't know why I even bother being nice to you. You just refuse to take good advice."

Miranda turned, stalked to the doorway, and dug an envelope out of her pocket. "Oh, here's your pay this month. There are only twenty weekdays in February so I prorated the cost down."

"Miranda, your bill I gave you last week has the correct amount. Also, you were late seven times this month in picking Cinderella up. There is a fee for that." Harper chased her to the door.

"You're here anyway," Miranda said with a sneer.

Taking a deep breath, Harper said the phrase she'd been practicing since last month. "I'm sorry your shop isn't making enough money, but the policy is the same for all parents. If you are late, there is a penalty."

"My shop is doing wonderfully," Miranda gasped with affront. "I'll bring you a check tomorrow."

"With an item that starts with D," Harper reminded her, trying to school her face not to smile as the unpleasant woman backed down like her mom had told her she would when they practiced.

"Fine."

"And Miranda? I already have a date for the reunion. Colt is taking me."

"Colt Ziegler? He hasn't been back for a reunion yet," Miranda stated with a skeptical look at Harper.

"This year, he'll be there. With me." Harper crossed two more fingers behind her back. *Please let him answer my message.*

"We'll see." Miranda let herself out the door.

Thank you for reading Coulda: A Second Chance For Mr. Right!

Don't miss future sweet and steamy Daddy stories by Pepper North? Subscribe to my newsletter!

I hope you'll enjoy this glimpse into Shoulda, the next story in the A Second Chance For Mr. Right series! You don't want to miss Harper and Colt's story.

Shoulda: A Second Chance For Mr. Right
Chapter One

Two weeks after high school graduation

Why won't she come with me?

Colt shoved his last pair of jeans into his suitcase. He was angry at her, angry at himself, and filled with self-doubt.

When a knock sounded at his bedroom door, he growled, "Leave me alone, Mom. You and Dad were very thorough in telling me all the reasons why I shouldn't believe in myself."

"I believe in you," a sweet voice observed, making him whirl around.

"Did you come to convince me not to go?" he asked angrily.

"No. I know you're going. You're supposed to go. I came to spend a few last minutes with you. I'm going to miss you so much," Harper shared, with tears in her eyes.

Colt shook his head, trying to maintain his resolve. He had to try this even though his heart felt like she was ripping it from his chest. He turned to grab some sock from the drawer and slammed it shut before turning to face her again.

"Then why the hell don't you come with me?" he demanded.

"I'll just hold you back," Harper whispered.

"That's bullshit and you know it. We're supposed to be together. You're supposed to be with me."

"How sure are you that going to Nashville is your path?" she asked, coming in to sit on his bed.

Immediately, he sat across from her on the opposite side of the double bed. "Four hundred percent."

"I believe you. I know this is what you have to do."

"Come with me," he asked, reaching for her hand and squeezing it gently.

"I can't, Colt. As confident as you are that you need to leave town and try to make it as a country superstar, I know my place is here," she told him.

"You could open a daycare anywhere," he assured her.

"I could, but I need to be here. I'm not like you. I'm... petrified of being in a new place I don't know how to get around in with no one I know to help me," she shared.

"I'd be there," he assured her.

"You would be. I know you'd always be there for me. Unfortunately, that will take your focus off doing what's important for you to succeed. We both know I'm great at a lot of things, but I'm too gullible."

"Kind-hearted," he corrected her.

She smiled at his editing. "I don't function well in crowds. My heart pounds and I want to cry. That won't go well with performing in front of a stadium of people."

Harper held her hand up when he opened his mouth to argue. "I might get better at being in public with you, but this isn't my dream. It's yours."

Colt stared at her for a second and digested her words. She was right. This was what he wanted. Her path was completely different. "I'm sorry, Harper. I'm an idiot."

"You are not. You're focused. That's what's going to help you make it big. I can't wait to see it happen. I am your biggest fan," she told him.

"You're so much more than that, Little girl."

"I can't be your Little girl, Colt. That's why I always say 'no' when you ask me out. You'll be a great Daddy to someone."

"You are my Little girl. We've been supposed to be together since before we even know the name for this bond between us. I'm not going to forget you. When you're ready to be mine, all you have to do is call. I will be there so fast there is burned rubber on the road into town."

"I can't count on you coming back, Colt. That's not fair to you. You need to go explore and live your life."

Harper looked around the room, seeming desperate for something as tears cascaded down her cheeks. Reading her mind, Colt bolted from the bed to snag a box of tissues from his desk and set it in front of her.

"I don't want you to cry, Harper. How can I make this better?"

"Fast forward twenty years or so. My heart will have recovered by then," she joked, wiping away the moisture under her eyes.

"You can always change your mind. I'll come get you," he promised her.

"Thanks. I'll remember that. I won't do it, but I'll remember you wanted me with you."

"Always. I'll always want you with me," he corrected her.
Harper dashed away a few tears and said, "You're leaving tomorrow?"

"Yes. I'll leave at eight in the morning. You can still change your mind and come with me. There's still time."

"I won't change my mind, Colt. It's not the best thing for me or for you."

Harper stood and took a step to the door before hesitating. She turned to face him. "Could I have a hug?"

"You're breaking my heart," he said, rushing around the bed to wrap his arms tightly around her. Unable to stop himself, he tangled his fingers in her hair and pulled her head back. Capturing her lips in a kiss that contained all his love for her and his frustration that they couldn't be together.

Her hands braced against his chest and Colt was ready to release her at her first move away. He'd never pushed himself on her and he never would. Her fingers grabbed his shirt. Colt felt the rasp of her fingernails through the fabric on his skin as Harper clung to him. Instantly, he was hard as he wrapped his other arm around her waist to pull her soft curves fully against him.

Colt memorized everything—her taste, the feel of her body against his, the way she responded to him. He was ready to call off his plans and stay here with her forever. He tightened his hold on her automatically when she shifted away.

"You have to let me go, Colt," she urged, tugging backward.

"I don't want to, Harper," he confessed before relaxing his arm around her waist.

"Sorry." He moved back six inches, searching her face to make sure he hadn't scared her.

"I wanted that kiss as much as you did, Colt. I'm going to miss you so much."

Covering her mouth with one hand, Harper whirled and dashed through the door. Colt automatically took several steps after her before bracing himself on the door frame to halt his progress. Chasing Harper would only make it harder and postpone the inevitable.

Want to read more? One click Shoulda: A Second Chance For Mr. Right to preorder now!

* * *

Read more from Pepper North

Dr. Richards' Littles®

A beloved age play series that features Littles who find their forever Daddies and Mommies. Dr. Richards guides and supports their efforts to keep their Littles happy and healthy.
Available on Amazon

Dr. Richards' Littles®
is a registered trademark of
With A Wink Publishing, LLC.
All rights reserved.

SANCTUM

Pepper North introduces you to an age play community that is isolated from the surrounding world. Here Littles can be Little, and Daddies can care for their Littles and keep them protected from the outside world.

Available on Amazon

Soldier Daddies

What private mission are these elite soldiers undertaking? They're all searching for their perfect Little girl.
Available on Amazon

The Keepers

This series from Pepper North is a twist on contemporary age play romances. Here are the stories of humans cared for by specially selected Keepers of an alien race. These are science fiction novels that age play readers will love!
Available on Amazon

The Magic of Twelve

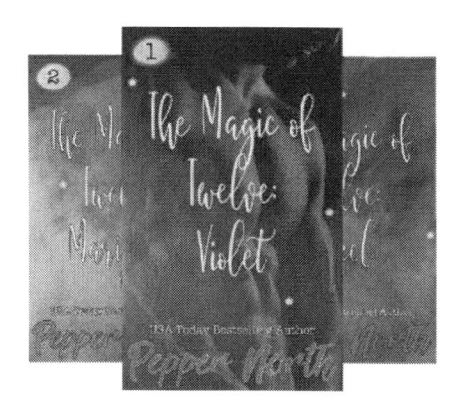

The Magic of Twelve features the stories of twelve women transported on their 22nd birthday to a new life as the droblin (cherished Little one) of a Sorcerer of Bairn. These magic wielders have waited a long time to take complete care of their droblin's needs. They will protect their precious one to their last drop of magic from a growing menace. Each novel is a complete story.

Available on Amazon

Ever just gone for it? That's what *USA Today* Bestselling Author Pepper North did in 2017 when she posted a book for sale on Amazon without telling anyone. Thanks to her amazing fans, the support of the writing community, Mr. North, and a killer schedule, she has now written more than 80 books!

Enjoy contemporary, paranormal, dark, and erotic romances that are both sweet and steamy? Pepper will convert you into one of her loyal readers. What's coming in the future? A Daddypalooza!

Sign up for Pepper North's newsletter

Like Pepper North on Facebook

Join Pepper's Readers' Group for insider information and giveaways!

Follow Pepper everywhere!

Amazon Author Page
BookBub
FaceBook
GoodReads
Instagram
TikToc
Twitter
YouTube
Visit Pepper's website for a current checklist of books!

Printed in Great Britain
by Amazon